MY SWEET

J. PHILLIPS

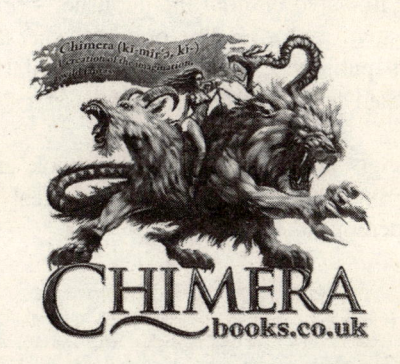

My Sweet Degradation first published in 2010 by
Chimera Books Ltd
PO Box 152
Waterlooville
Hants
PO8 9FS

Printed and bound in Great Britain by
Cox & Wyman, Reading.

978-1-903931-90-5

This novel is fiction – in real life practice safe sex

This book is sold subject to the condition that it shall not, by way of trade or otherwise, be lent, resold, hired out or otherwise circulated without the publisher's prior written consent in any form of binding or cover other than that in which it is published, and without a similar condition being imposed on the subsequent purchaser.

The characters and situations in this book are entirely imaginary and bear no relation to any real person or actual happening.

Copyright © J. Phillips

The right of J. Phillips to be identified as author of this book has been asserted in accordance with section 77 and 78 of the Copyrights Designs and Patents Act 1988.

MY SWEET DEGRADATION

J. Phillips

Chimera *(kī-mîr'ə, kĭ-)* a creation of the imagination, a wild fantasy

Contents

A Little Lesson in Respect	5
A Very Naughty Girl Indeed	30
My Sweet Degradation	53
Do Not Disturb	81
A Bad Girl's Revenge	101
Intensive Care	125
The Discipline Officer	175
The Erotic Advancement of Little Red	198

A Little Lesson in Respect

'Spoilt, little bitch,' that's what he'd called me, and you know what, given the way I would behave back then, I don't suppose he was far wrong – behaving like a brat seemed to have come as an unfortunate side-effect to me growing up in a wealthy family. I'm much better now – well, most of the time anyway – and who knows, perhaps that all comes down to that hot summer's evening when I was finally taught a little lesson in respect.

I knew fine well that I was going to be late, but I'm afraid it didn't concern me in the slightest. Gently tugging on the reins so that Charlie turned into the dusty, birch-lined avenue that led back towards the stables, I couldn't help but notice how my shiny new Range Rover – a birthday present from daddy – was now the last, lonely occupant of an otherwise deserted car park. As I went on to guide my horse carefully across the cobbled courtyard, newly hosed down and shining like polished marble in the setting sunlight, I actually began to wonder if they'd forgotten all about us and had shut up shop for the evening. It was a foolish notion, of course, as I should have known fine well that there was at least one man who would not be able to relax until he knew that every single horse was bedded down and left comfortable for the evening.

Rounding the final corner I spotted him. He was standing over by one of the heavy water butts, facing away and oblivious to our presence. Clearly he was in the last stages of changing from work clothes into civvies, as he stood shirtless in jeans and boots only. I watched his semi-naked form with an illicit excitement tingling goose-bumps across my upper arms, as he bent to retrieve a white linen shirt from his bag, casually buttoning it across his lithe, sun-kissed torso before rolling the sleeves to the elbows. All of a sudden he looked over his shoulder to catch me staring, and immediately he set off with a determination in his step that forewarned of his anger.

Patrick was the stable manager, notorious for being something of a loner and for caring more about the animals in his charge than any human being in his life. Rumour had it that when younger he'd spent a life in and out of trouble with the law, and had even done a short stint in prison for some misdemeanour or other. It was supposedly through him being given a community order sentence for brawling that he'd found himself working at the stables in the first place. Quite by accident a mutual rapport with the horses was discovered and he was duly taken on as a live-in stable boy, thus bringing to an end his life of petty crime. Anyway, Patrick was a grown man now and a rather handsome one with it. I would be lying if I said I hadn't paid him quiet attention in the past, but as he was so far removed from the world in which I moved I wouldn't have even begun to view him as anything more than a pleasant fantasy to indulge in while waiting for Charlie to be made ready.

Despite his all-too-evident frustration, Patrick looked just as good as ever. He had what I guess some might call a 'real man' attractiveness about him – strong, natural good-looks with one or two rough edges that suited him well. But what really did it for me were those milky-blue eyes, which displayed a brooding intensity with the power to both unnerve and excite at the same time. There was definitely something animalistic about him, and together with his short dark hair, and permanent two-day beard growth, he could be a rather unnerving presence to behold. Although – and perhaps it was only a product of my imagination – on those rare occasions when I managed to observe him unnoticed, I wondered if I could detect a sadder, lonelier side to him. Perhaps it was this facet of his personality that the animals could sense, where most people were blind beyond his considerable physical presence. I don't know. In that instant, however, as I watched him clench his fists in a way that caused the veins in his forearms to pop, there was absolutely no sign of a placid side.

'You're late!' he snapped, looking up at me through furrowed brow as he snatched the reins from my grip and stroked a hand across Charlie's neck to soothe him as though we'd been missing for days on end.

'Oh, am I really?' I replied with a smirk, it never having been in my nature to apologise. 'Oops!'

Patrick squinted up at me against the glare of

the setting sun, the first tiny creases spreading out from the corners of his eyes to mark a life spent working outdoors. 'I suppose you think I've nowhere better to be; that I'm here simply to serve you?' he continued, and I couldn't help but grin at his outburst.

I swung a leg across Charlie's back, momentarily popping my riding crop between my teeth and cheekily placing a hand on Patrick's muscular shoulder for support as I dropped to the ground before him. He scowled and guided the horse to a nearby water trough, tying the reins to a post and softly encouraging him to drink before turning to face me once more. I had lost my position of physical domination now and the stable manager towered over me by a good six or seven inches. Over the years I'd learnt other ways to unnerve a man, however, and I slowly ran my gaze over the contours of his chest, smiling with raised eyebrows, but Patrick only ignored me and returned to his tirade.

'Just because *daddy* pays all that money so his precious little princess can stable her horse here you think you can do just about anything you like, don't you?'

I'd never heard anything like it: he'd spat the word 'daddy' as though it left a nasty taste in the mouth and, good-looking or not, his attitude actually began to annoy me. Me being me, however, I only countered with an indignant aggression of my own.

'Well yes, to be quite frank. If it wasn't for my

father and his *precious little princess* you would be out of a job and back to stealing cars – or whatever the hell it is people like you get up to – so perhaps you should show me a little more respect in future. I could have you fired for speaking to me in such a way.'

He narrowed his eyes further and stared hard within my own, gritting his teeth and tensing his jaw as he tried and then failed to keep his fury in check. 'You spoilt little bitch,' he hissed, and without thinking I lashed out, giving in to my short temper as I swung at him. The severity of my action was immediately made clear by the loud crack as the leather tip of my riding crop made cruel contact with the stubbled flesh of his cheek.

But Patrick barely flinched, and simply stood in silence, slowly bringing up his fingertips to carefully test the wound that now marked a vulgar diagonal across his skin. His stare once more gripped me, only this time with an icy anger that caused my stomach to lurch with fear for the reprisal I instinctively knew was to come.

'Oh God, I'm sorry, I... I didn't mean to...' I quickly began, but the time for apologies was clearly long gone. Yelping with fright I felt the crop suddenly ripped from my fingers, yet that was nothing compared to my horror as I watched Patrick suddenly lunge forward, bending at the knees so that his shoulder slammed hard into my tummy and the wind was knocked from my lungs.

Before I could make sense of what was going

on I felt myself lifted entirely from the ground. An arm snaked its way around the back of my knees to hold me tight as I was tossed effortlessly over his shoulder.

'What... what the fuck...?' I cried, when I could draw enough breath to protest, my defensive anger renewed. But Patrick simply spun on his heels and marched forward without reply. 'What the hell do you think you're doing?' I demanded, as the stable manager's shoulder dug uncomfortably into the muscles of my stomach with every heavy step he took.

'Put me down!' I cried, balling my fists and hammering them over and over against his back. 'Put me down this instant!' It was little more than a waste of my energy, however, as Patrick did not react in the slightest. I tried to kick out too, but the way in which he carried me meant I could make no contact whatsoever and my legs flailed uselessly in the air.

Through the thick mist of confusion the blood surged noisily within my ears. I distinctly recall breathing in the warm, sticky-sweet scent of fresh hay a split-second before Patrick came to a halt and I felt myself thrown backwards. I cried out in anticipation of pain to come, yet only found myself falling into a bed of soft straw, flinching as I watched him toss my riding crop down alongside me.

Drawing short, desperate breaths through my nostrils I scrambled to my feet to confront the man before me.

'How dare you?' I shouted, but it was Patrick's

turn to smirk now. 'What on earth do you think you're doing?'

He had brought me into the hay barn, a beautiful old building far too draughty to house the expensive thoroughbreds the stables catered for these days, yet far too charming to be pulled down. I could see that I would have to push beyond him in order to make my way to the open doors, and I suppose I ought to have been frightened, but between the adrenaline that coursed through my veins and my youthful arrogance, all I felt was rage.

I stepped to the side and forward, yet he just grinned and moved with me to block my escape. I clawed my hands towards him and cursed, but he only laughed and quickly ducked aside, smoothly taking my wrists in his strong, calloused hands to hold me at bay. Finally, as I tried in vain to free myself from his vicelike grip, the gravity of my predicament began to dawn and I released a tiny whimper of frustration. 'Why... why are you doing this?' I questioned pathetically, but before I had a chance to say more Patrick suddenly forced his bodyweight forward so that I had no option but to stagger back until my shoulder slammed hard into a gnarled oak pillar that rose vertically from the ground.

Quickly he adjusted his grip to hold both of my wrists in one hand only, and once more I tried to wrench myself free. Even then I was no match for his strength and all I could do was watch as he reached up to take a coil of rope that hung from a rusted nail above my head. Struggle as I might it was useless and my panic rose with a prickly heat. Slowly and deliberately Patrick began to wind one end of the rope around and around my wrists.

'Please...' I pleaded weakly, desperately trying to pull away, but he only continued with his work, eventually tying the rope off in a knot. He then took a step or two back and smirked at me, unfurling the rope as he went. Suddenly he gave a sharp tug so that my arms were yanked forward and I had no choice but to stumble towards him. My enforced compliance obviously amused him no end, as he threw back his head and laughed in response.

'T-tell me, please, what are you doing?' I begged once more, my throat dry, my eyes welling with tears of frustration.

'Well it's very simple really,' he offered, all too casually. 'I'm going to teach you a little lesson. If you're so fond of attacking people then it's only fair you get a taste of your own medicine, now isn't it?'

Never before had anyone dared to treat me in such a manner and my mind reeled with a confused mix of fear and anger. With another tug Patrick forced me to stagger even further forward until I stood pretty much in the centre of the barn. Through stinging eyes I watched as he effortlessly tossed his end of the rope up and over an exposed beam that spanned the entire length of the old barn, before leaning down to retrieve it once more.

Again he wound the rope in, only this time I was horrified to feel my arms being pulled vertically up above my head.

Perhaps his delight in my anguish had caught him off guard as, noticing he'd inadvertently stepped a little closer to me, and seeing it as a last chance to get away, I seized the moment and kicked out with all my might, the toe of my riding boot making sharp contact with his shin.

'Jesus!' he cursed. 'You little bitch!' and leaning down to soothe his wound he released his hold on the rope, whereupon I quickly made a dash for the open barn doors.

But my attempt at escape was all too short-lived as, with a grunted, 'Oh no you fucking don't,' Patrick quickly dived and grabbed at the loose end of rope as it snaked its way up towards the beam, throwing his entire bodyweight against it so that I was suddenly brought up short and the dry fibres bit painfully into my wrists.

'So, it's going to be like that, is it?' he spat as he limped towards me, winding the rope round and round his palm with slow menace, forcing me to stagger, step by step, into the centre of the barn where my arms were yet again stretched up above my head. 'I guess if you're gonna kick like a stubborn donkey then we'd better tether you like one, hadn't we?'

'No!' I gasped. 'Really, I'm sorry, please.'

I stared in terror, my heart pounding as Patrick scanned the barn, presumably looking for more rope to bind my legs with, but then, all of a sudden, his eyes fixed upon me once more and his grimace slowly stretched into a cruel smile that caused a shiver to run the length of my spine.

'Well, it looks as though we're all out of rope,' he whispered, stepping a little closer. 'But not to worry; there *is* another way of keeping those lovely legs of yours in place.' I couldn't imagine what on earth he was talking about, and I nibbled anxiously at my lower lip as I awaited his next move.

Patrick once more came within striking distance, and for an instant I actually considered kicking out again, but at the last moment he yanked hard upon his end of the rope so that I had no option but to squeal and stretch up on tiptoe to ease the biting squeeze on my wrists.

Quickly he stepped into me, his chest pressing against my breasts and his hand unceremoniously gripping my jaw. He twisted my head to the side and I was forced to take anxious breaths through my nostrils as he repeated into my ear, 'There *is* another way.'

Patrick relaxed his hold on the rope so I could once more stand on the flats of my feet. He hardly moved back, however, and I was given no chance to settle my nerves as I suddenly became aware of fingers clawing, without care or subtlety, at the waistband of my riding breeches. Naturally I drew breath to protest, but all I could manage was a shocked, 'No!' a split-second before I felt him wrench down with all his strength. Two press-studs offered no resistance whatsoever and the thin zipper gave just as easily. With three, or perhaps four, awkward tugs more Patrick had my breeches down over my boots to leave them bunched uselessly around my ankles. And he was quite right; there was no way on earth that I could kick at him now, and through my natural reflex to pull away I immediately lost my balance, which Patrick corrected by leaning on the rope so that, with a distressed cry, I was lifted back into a standing position once more.

It was more through observing his reaction, rather than any realisation of my own, that the true nature of my exposure now became apparent. You see, back then I wouldn't always wear underwear while riding. My breeches were obviously the finest money could buy and offered perfect protection and comfort. Panties weren't really necessary, and at times I would enjoy the extra freedom of sitting that little 'closer' in the saddle. Tied up as I was, with arms stretched painfully above my head, I couldn't really see below the swell of my breasts, yet that sudden look of doubt on Patrick's face, the way he swallowed awkwardly and took a single, faltering step back, was all I needed to be reminded that my neat little pussy – waxed, but for a thin strip of silky curls rising upward – was now his to behold.

An itchy heat flooded my cheeks. It wasn't so much that I was bashful – I had always been rather proud of my body and perhaps a little too happy to show it off at times – it was more that my vulnerability was now expressed in a new, more dangerous way, and I found myself wondering exactly what the ex-criminal might be capable of.

Because of the sticky heat of the day I had chosen to wear a black cotton vest only above my riding breeches, which, with it barely falling below my cute belly button, did absolutely nothing towards protecting my modesty.

As I looked up once again it was plain to see by the change in Patrick's expression that he too was aware of the shift in the already highly charged atmosphere of the barn, and I suspect that if I'd been careful, if I'd made use of my natural cunning, I might have been able to make him back down. But of course I was young, foolish and headstrong back then, and as a result I only succeeded in committing my gravest error so far.

'Oh please let me go,' I implored. 'I'm sorry. I shouldn't have hit you. And you're right; it was rude of me to come back so late. Maybe if I was to pay you – as an apology for your wasted time, I mean? My purse is in the car. If you would just untie me, I... I don't think I have a huge amount of cash, but there might be thirty or forty—' My plaintive words suddenly ended in a pained squeal as the rope was yanked tight once more.

'Well isn't that fucking typical?' he snorted with renewed disdain. 'The little rich girl thinks she can buy her way out of trouble in just the same way she buys everything else. Well, *little rich girl*,' he continued, sneering, taking a step closer and wrapping another coil of rope around his hand to stretch me to my extreme, 'how much is it worth? How much for hitting and kicking me? How much for me having to stay back late for you time and time again just because you think you're more important than anyone else? How much should you pay me for the trouble you cause when you change out of your riding gear in the full knowledge that the stable boys are watching you, and so I can't get them to concentrate on a fucking thing afterwards?'

I felt my cheeks flush a little deeper.

'How much money are you going to give me not to teach you the lesson you should have been taught years ago? One hundred? Two hundred?' All the time he spoke he'd been stepping closer and closer until he stood right before me, his eyes burning with a violent rage.

'No,' he said after a slight pause, and with a newfound calm that was even more unnerving than his anger, 'not this time. This time even money won't help you.'

Patrick quickly turned away and I watched in petrified silence as he bent smoothly from the waist to sweep my riding crop from the hay-strewn floor. He swished it first one way and then the other, testing its action so that the sultry evening air whistled mockingly against the leather tip and I was forced to offer a panicked, 'Oh no, please,' in response.

But my pleas clearly meant nothing to him, as he merely stepped around me, avoiding my gaze as he went.

In the end I'm not sure what was worse; the

moment of silence that stretched into an eternity – my heart fit to burst as I sensed him, watching me, assessing me from behind – or the sudden touch of crop against flesh, which caused me to tense my every muscle and to gasp as it traced slowly over the contours of one naked buttock and then down across the other. Of course Patrick was only taunting me, enjoying his own game in the knowledge that I would have been expecting nothing but pain.

That pain did come all too soon, however. A loud dry crack that ripped through the silence of the barn, causing me to cry out and my knees to buckle as a white-hot agony set my nerves alight. I prayed that my ordeal was finally over – an eye-for-an-eye, a strike-for-a-strike – but my hopes were quickly dashed as Patrick swept the leather tip of the crop down against me once more, only this time with a backhand swipe against the opposite cheek.

'Oh Jesus!' I screamed as he whipped me again and again, first one buttock and then the other. 'Please, no! I'm sorry! Stop it; stop it please!' Yet my begging only seemed to make him thrash me all the harder until my tortured flesh burned with a stinging pain worse than any I'd experienced before. With each pitiless bite of the crop I would cry out and attempt to pull away, but there was absolutely nowhere for me to hide: Patrick held firmly onto his end of the rope so that I had no choice but to stand upright, and my legs were as good as shackled by my riding breeches gathered clumsily around my ankles.

The best I could manage was to tense and release the muscles of my bottom, twisting from one side to the other, but it offered me no relief whatsoever.

Hot salty tears spilled down over my cheeks. They were tears like none I'd ever known before, and I can only assume they stemmed from the intense, nagging frustration that caused me to grit my teeth and dig my perfectly manicured nails into the soft flesh of my palms. It was a frustration that made me draw short breaths through my nostrils and to release deep sobs from the back of my throat.

Patrick's punishment was relentless, and no matter how much I pleaded he continued to flog me without mercy.

But then, just as I thought I could take it no more, a strange thing happened. Somehow the pain seemed to solidify, it became less unbearable in a truly physical sense, but more so in the way that it left me with an unexplainable longing, a longing that gnawed at my nerves and could only be momentarily satisfied by the next cruel lick of leather against skin. I continued to cry out with every vicious impact of the crop, but somehow differently, and in a way that I could make no real sense of.

In time, and through a whirl of confused emotions, I noticed that the severity of the thrashing had diminished. He was still using the crop against me with the same rhythmical efficiency as before, yet a little lighter now, and with an upward motion only against the lower curve of my ass cheeks – first one side and then the other.

I found myself tensing and releasing those muscles, and desperately trying to understand my body's reaction to the torture, I tested my senses with every strike, noticing how he would follow through with the crop, running it against my burning flesh in a way that soothed it with the gentlest caress of the soft leather tongue, and shocking though the realisation was, I couldn't help but love it.

Patrick slowly began to release coil after coil of rope from around his hand, and I certainly took advantage of the freedom in my arms to relax them a little. But rather peculiarly, and somewhat shamefully, I also found myself bending forward from the waist, lower and lower, and in a way that I can only retrospectively accept came from a secret desire to feel the crop's touch more intimately still.

The stable manager seemed to understand my need and I gasped, feeling an icy shiver run through my body, as the tip of the riding crop pressed just above my knee to slowly caress its way upward.

'Oh, God!' I moaned as the smooth cool leather traced ever so lightly against the swell of my hairless pussy for all too brief a moment, before moving on to gently run down my other thigh. Another length of rope was released and still lower I bent, shuffling my legs apart as best I could to offer myself more blatantly still, and again Patrick brought the crop between my thighs, drawing the tip lightly back and forth against the contours of my slit.

'So you like that, do you?' he drawled, and I recoiled at the smug satisfaction in his voice. If he had simply wanted to punish me then all he needed do was to stop right there, right then – to leave me lost in that state of pure physical yearning – yet he did no such thing. Whether it was through the thrill he was gaining by witnessing me debase myself so thoroughly, or because of his own swelling arousal I will never know, but Patrick continued to work the crop against me, pressing still deeper so that the shaft parted my lips and its subtly undulating surface rubbed back and forth against my clit.

'Oh,' I gasped again, and Patrick released a snort of derisive laughter in response.

'So, I see you're not just a spoilt little bitch, but you're a dirty slut too,' he mocked, and the humiliation once more surged within me. Ordinarily I wouldn't have dreamt of allowing anyone to speak to me in such a way, and despite the fact that I was in no position to do so – tied up as I was – there was still a tiny reflex that told me to fight. Of course I did nothing of the sort, partly because I was all but beyond rational thought, but also, and rather disturbingly, there was something that excited me about the way that he had the nerve to insult me so vulgarly.

'Maybe you need whipping here too,' he continued, and I felt the crop draw back until the leather tongue rested on my clit. 'Maybe I should beat you just here for offering your body so flagrantly to lowlife scum like me.'

'Oh yes,' I hissed as Patrick began to gently spank my pussy with the tip of the riding crop. He didn't use it aggressively against me, nor in a way designed to cause real pain, but he would hit me just hard enough to send tiny spasms of pleasure firing throughout my body, forcing me to twist my hips one way and then the other so that his strikes would land just where I needed to feel them.

'You really are a bad little girl, aren't you?' he sneered, now sawing the crop back and forth between my slick pussy lips.

'No... no I'm not,' I panted, but deep down I was discovering that he was absolutely right.

'Really?' he replied with overly-dramatic surprise, the tip of the crop again taunting the swell of my mound with gentle, repetitive slaps. 'Well if you were a good girl then surely you wouldn't be bending over and showing-off that tight little cunt of yours to a lowly stable worker like me – to a man your father pays to serve you. Surely only a bad girl would do that. Or am I wrong?' The leather tongue began to caress deeper, to run ever so lightly across that other little hole of mine, and I couldn't help but gasp.

'N-no, you're wrong,' I stammered weakly, stubbornly drawing on whatever vestiges of pride I could muster.

Then Patrick suddenly tossed the riding crop down and, with raised voice he said, 'I think we can add *liar* to the list alongside *spoilt* and *dirty*. If you're really not just a little slut then how do you explain this?' His hand quickly slid between my thighs, the tip of a single finger working its way between my pussy lips to slip so easily within. Reflexively I tightened my muscles around him and moaned as he curved against the natural contours of my body.

'So you're not a bad girl then?' he sneered, fucking me with his finger before withdrawing once more. 'You're not a dirty little slut? Next you'll be telling me this isn't, in fact, *your* juices I see smeared all over my hand. What do you think?'

Before I could respond he reached his arm around my shoulder, taking my chin in his hand and forcing his sticky finger inside my mouth. I bit down defensively, but this only made him squeeze my cheeks painfully so that I had no option but to relax my jaw once more.

'So you want to nip like a donkey too, do you?' he laughed, grabbing my hair with the hand that still held onto the rope and easing my head back while he proceeded to smear first my tongue and then my lips with my own traitorous juices.

'I suppose if you weren't a slut then you wouldn't be desperate for me to fuck you either, would you?' he mocked.

'I'm not!' I insisted, still unwilling to own up to the shameful truth, and I listened with both fear and a trembling excitement to the sound of his belt buckle being released, and his jeans being drawn down. 'Please!' I squealed.

'You're a liar,' he hissed, and I couldn't help

but cry out as I felt the swollen head of his cock press into the sensitive flesh of my pussy. 'You're a liar and a dirty little rich bitch.'

He worked his bulbous helmet against my entrance and my body betrayed me all too easily. I had no doubt that he would be able to thrust into me without any difficulty whatsoever, and closing my eyes I prepared myself for just that outcome...

'But maybe you're right and I've read you all wrong,' he goaded, as he drew the head of his stiff prick up and down my slit, to mock me with my own wetness. 'I've done some pretty bad things in the past, but I've never forced myself on a woman. We both know what you really want, but I'm not gonna give it to you until you ask me to.'

The stable manager pressed against me once more, and reflexively I angled my hips to meet him, willing him to enter me fully, but just at the point where I felt certain he was about to slip deep inside he pulled back again and I was forced to whimper my frustration.

'Say it,' he hissed. 'Tell me you want me to fuck you.'

But I couldn't allow myself to give him that satisfaction.

Once again he tugged my hair so that my head was wrenched uncomfortably back, but it somehow only served to intensify the bittersweet sensation of his prick teasing me from behind, tight between my thighs, gently pumping back and forth against my wet pussy lips.

My mind battled with the desperate need for pure physical satisfaction, and the knowledge that I was demeaning myself so disgracefully, and I took desperate breaths through my nostrils, swallowing through a constricted throat.

'Say it,' he growled. 'Tell me and I'll give you just what you want.'

'No, please...' I gasped, wincing as he wound his roped hand still deeper into my hair. Again I tried to push back, to make him fuck me without me having to lower myself by begging him, but once more he pulled away.

'Say it. Tell me to fuck you like the dirty little slut you are, and I'll let you feel my stiff cock slide all the way inside your cunt.' My eyes filled with fresh tears of humiliation and finally, unable to take his taunting any longer, I gave in.

'All right,' I whispered, utterly broken.

'All right what?' he tormented.

'Look, please,' I pleaded, 'just fuck me.'

It was a bliss-filled agony to feel him teasing my pussy entrance in such a way; pushing into me, over and over, so that his swollen helmet would stretch me wide yet never quite enter. Looking back I suppose it must have been just as physically tortuous for him as it was for me, and I do wonder if he would simply have fucked me in the end, no matter what, but to my shame that was an eventuality we never met.

'Say it properly and you can have what you want. Tell me you're a spoilt little bitch and you want me to fuck you.'

Again the tears overflowed. He had won and

he was right; I *was* a spoilt little bitch and really did want him to fuck me. So with a deep, shivering breath I did as I was told. 'Yes, yes I am,' I whispered, my submissive obedience thrilling me even further. 'I'm a spoilt little bitch. Now fuck me, *please…*'

And Patrick finally gave me what I yearned for, with one powerful movement thrusting deep to sink the entire length of his beautiful prick deep within me.

'Oh!' I sobbed, the sudden, overwhelming sense of satisfaction causing my head to swim and my inner muscles to clutch around the intrusion. But all too soon he began to withdraw, and I released a tiny cry of frustration as he pulled away. For an instant I actually feared he might leave me for good, that he was not yet done with his teasing, but then he sank into me again, harder and deeper this time while releasing a guttural cry of his own.

Patrick fucked me good and hard from behind. It was sex as raw and as animalistic as I have ever experienced, and I cried out with each electrifying thrill that rippled through my body. Beyond the physical pleasure I drew illicit satisfaction from the shameful knowledge that I had been tied up against my will, stripped as good as naked, and all so that the stable manager might abuse my body by way of a punishment.

In and out he pumped – harder and faster. His hands clawed at the tortured flesh of my ass cheeks, squeezing and drawing them apart to expose me more intimately still, and I cursed vulgarly with every powerful thrust of his hips, every slap of his groin against my buttocks, the rope burning my wrists as I leant into its biting grip for support.

I knew I'd not be unable to hold out for much longer, that my body was rapidly being drawn towards something colossal, and I forced myself to try and relax so as to extend the pleasure for as long as possible, but it was no good; the relentless pounding of his thick shaft alongside the extreme sexual tension that had grown within me from the moment Patrick had tossed me over his shoulder, meant I was fighting a losing battle.

And so it happened. Panting wildly I felt my orgasm suddenly surge with a molten heat. 'Oh fuck, oh fuck, oh fuck,' I gasped, my legs buckling so that Patrick was forced to quickly wrap a strong arm around my waist as I surrendered completely. Over and over again I cried out, my climax crashing down on me in a succession of waves. And through it all Patrick fucked me just as perfectly as ever, only with shorter, more aggressive strokes, and as my body inevitably began to slow he succumbed to his own pleasure.

Perhaps it was meant as a final act of degradation, maybe it was simply how he liked it, but as I felt his muscles lock tight, as I listened to his breath catch at the back of his throat, he suddenly withdrew from my replete body and releasing an anguished growl, he spurted hot sticky seed all over my ravished bottom – a final insult to 'daddy's little princess'.

In time that inevitable cold realisation, where irrational desire is superseded by rational thought, took hold, and the blood once again rose to my cheeks. Patrick must have experienced something similar as I suddenly felt the rope slacken completely, so that I could finally lower my aching arms to my sides.

I listened, without daring to turn around, to the sound of him pulling up and fastening his jeans. He then stepped around to the front of me and I watched as his fingers carefully worked at the knotted rope around my wrists. Once or twice I dared to look up at his face, yet he refused to meet my gaze, his expression remaining inscrutable. The rope eventually came loose and he quickly unwound it before allowing it to fall to the ground.

To say that the atmosphere in the barn was awkward would be an understatement of epic proportions, but what possible, comfortable resolution could there have been? Of course there was none, and in the end it was all I could do to watch as the stable manager turned away and headed purposefully towards the open doors.

For some bizarre reason I felt the desire to call out to him before he left, but to say exactly what I wasn't sure. An apology, perhaps? Or a thank you? And then it was too late anyway; Patrick was gone, his silhouette swallowed by the gathering dusk outside.

As for me, I just stood there, wiping my tear-streaked cheeks against the hem of my top before awkwardly bending down to pull my breeches up with numb fingers and thumbs. I felt utterly spent. My backside burnt with a pain I had momentarily forgotten, and the sticky residue of his sperm trickled down a thigh as I refastened the press studs at my waist.

I tried to make sense of what had just happened, of what the stable manager had done to me and, more shockingly, of what I had begged him to do, but I only ended up confusing myself further.

Yes he had humiliated me, yes he had inflicted pain on my body worse than anything I had experienced before, but I had accepted it, craved it even, and it pushed me to behave in ways I never thought possible.

Stepping out into the courtyard I saw no sign of either Patrick or Charlie, yet I had no doubt that wherever they were they would be there together, each one happy in the other's company. I suddenly felt incredibly alone, and as I walked back towards my car I reflected that I really could behave like a spoilt brat at times, and that perhaps I should try treating people a little better. I suppose it would be easy to suggest that such a revelation came as a direct result of Patrick punishing me like he did, but personally, I'm not so sure. I have a feeling it was more to do with that profound sense of loneliness after an act so intimate.

Either way it didn't matter, as the end result was just the same; it was time for me to grow up.

A Very Naughty Girl Indeed

The PE teacher had already buzzed ahead to warn me that she was sending over a naughty young lady in need of punishment. What she had failed to inform me of, however, was the reason *why* you were in trouble.

In the end I could easily have lost my job for the punishment I chose for you. Christ, let's be honest, I really *should* have lost my job for the punishment I chose for you.

There was a knock at the door...

'Come!' I called, and tentatively you stepped into my office.

You were still dressed in your gym clothes: a tight, powder-blue top showing-off the contours of your firm breasts just perfectly. Below you wore a tiny gymslip that displayed far too much of your naked thighs, and on your feet a simple pair of white training shoes.

You looked good. You looked *too* good.

It wasn't always easy being the head of the school, you know; particularly when I had to discipline naughty sixth-form girls. Particularly when I had to discipline naughty sixth-form girls like you. Yes, you were a young woman, but I was your headmaster and from the very first moment that the thought had entered my mind I knew I was lost.

I could feel my prick beginning to swell as I stared at you standing nervously before me.

'So, young lady, what have you been up to this time?' I asked, and in response you just dropped your head and stared down at your feet, your cheeks flushing a rosy pink.

'Well come on, girl, I don't have all day!' Briefly you looked up at me through glossy eyes to offer an inaudible mumble, before staring down once more.

'Oh for goodness' sake girl, speak up! I doubt anything you've done this time could be any worse than your previous indiscretions, now could it?' How wrong could I be?

Finally you looked up once more, your eyes piercing my own with the defiance of youth as you spoke in a full, clear voice. 'Miss Jones caught me masturbating in the changing rooms, sir.'

It was my turn to blush now. I stared down at my desk, pointlessly shuffling papers from one side to the next and swallowing hard through a dry, constricted throat. Embarrassment wasn't the only emotion flooding my senses, however, and a second, much more powerful reaction began to exert itself. My cock stood fully erect inside my trousers and throbbed with an immoral desire at the thought of the beautiful young woman before me playing with herself when she thought no one was watching. I knew then for certain that I simply had to have you, and drew a deep breath in a somewhat futile attempt to calm myself and retain my necessarily austere demeanour.

Forcing myself to reassert the appearance of

authority once more, I spoke again. 'I see. Well, a young lady of your age should barely know of such things, let alone be performing them during school hours. You do realise I will have to punish you, don't you?' And timidly you nodded your head.

I had always prided myself on a sense of creativity where disciplining wayward pupils was concerned. Perhaps in this instance, however, I was a little *too* creative.

'As you know, I believe it is appropriate to punish guilty students in a way that somehow reflects the crime they have committed. Remember that time you were caught littering and I made you clean the entire schoolyard?' Again, a wordless nod. 'Well, I'm going to follow that principal now; if you enjoy touching yourself so much then you can demonstrate exactly what you've been up to, now, to me.'

'But, sir…' you suddenly protested and really, you were right to do so.

'No buts, young lady. My mind is quite made up. Now, pull over that chair, remove your underwear and sit down. I want to see what you find so stimulating about that body of yours.'

I watched, taking secret satisfaction in your all-too-evident discomfort, as you remained standing still in the centre of the office, staring at the floor while your cheeks burnt a deeper shade of red.

'Good God, girl! Must I do everything for you?'

Standing up – my erection tenting the front of my suit trousers, but thankfully your eyes were firmly fixed to the floor – I walked around to the front of my desk and dragged across a low armchair until it was positioned next to you.

'Lift up your skirt,' I scolded, and with nervous hands you did exactly as you were told, to reveal white cotton knickers that moulded snugly to the contour of your mound, the vertical line of your slit obvious beneath the thin fabric.

Slipping my fingers beneath the elastic waistband I quickly, and unceremoniously, peeled down your panties to expose what has to be one of the prettiest pussies I have ever seen.

'What's this?' I questioned with feigned anger. 'Have you been shaving your puss... your vagina, young lady?'

'Waxing, sir,' you replied, in a voice barely more than a whisper.

'Well, I'm starting to see what a truly naughty girl you are, and I wonder if merely making you recreate your deviant act will not nearly be enough of a punishment.'

I couldn't, could I? In that instant I pictured myself bending you over my desk and sliding my rigid prick inside that beautiful little cunt of yours, but it would surely have meant me losing my job.

I wet my lips, my cock pleading to be released, and stepped back behind the desk to retake my seat.

'All right then, young lady, go ahead,' I ordered, concentrating on keep my voice level and authoritative. 'Show me exactly what you were caught doing in the changing rooms by

Miss Jones.'

I stared, utterly enrapt, as finally you complied, slipping out of your panties entirely and sitting down on the very front edge of the chair. I revelled in your embarrassment, your eyes glossy and on the brink of tears, cheeks ablaze with shame, as slowly you leant back.

'Well come along, girl,' I prompted, 'part your legs.' And you did so.

Your sweet pussy was so rudely exposed to me now, yet still I needed to see more.

'Goodness, young lady, wider!' I chastised. 'Hook your legs over the arms of the chair!'

And it was a remarkable sight to behold as you obeyed me completely, slowly lifting your thighs, one after the other, until the backs of your knees folded over either armrest. You slid your toned bottom even further to the very edge of the chair and your flushed, pink sex lips separated at the last moment to display a thin, silken line of moisture within.

It was no good; I could not watch such an entrancing, illicit display without enjoying a little pleasure of my own – but that would be the end of it, I tried to convince myself.

Carefully, and entirely hidden from you by my desk, I unzipped my fly and withdrew my angry, swollen cock, taking it tightly within a fist.

'Okay, that's better,' I managed, my throat feeling tight with emotion. 'Now, touch yourself just as you did when you were caught by Miss Jones.'

With only the briefest of hesitations you

reached a hand between your spread thighs, and with two fingers you began to slowly and awkwardly touch yourself. You shut your eyes tightly, through embarrassment or pleasure I could not tell.

The sight of you stroking that perfectly smooth pussy was something unbelievably special, and I began to pump my shaft harder still. 'Come now,' I admonished, 'do it properly. I know *exactly* how naughty young ladies masturbate, you know, and I can assure you that one day you will thank me for this punishment.'

These words seemed to finally switch something in your mind, and you gasped and relaxed that little further back into the chair. Giving in to the moment you began to nibble pensively your lower lip, while clearly teasing yourself in just the way you liked to.

Glistening fingers slid up and down your naked slit, smearing and stretching your soft flesh in every direction before you finally allowed them to seek out that tiny fold of flesh and to play with your swollen clit directly. You circled it round and round, teased it up and down and from side to side, sometimes quickly and sometimes slowly, and I watched in awe as your tight body began to twitch and jerk with each increasingly powerful spasm that exploded from within.

Whilst surreptitiously continuing to fuck my fist from behind the cover of my desk I suddenly realised that you might actually allow yourself to orgasm in front of me, right there, on the armchair, in my office. I could easily have done so too, but, wonderful though the prospect was, I knew deep down that I could not possibly allow that to happen.

Moaning now from the back of your throat, your hips began to rise and fall with a constant pulsating rhythm, giving themselves completely to the unremitting tease of your fingers. Without any prompting from me your free hand slipped down between your thighs also and I felt my cock jerk violently as I watched you work a single finger between your pussy lips to fuck your entrance with short, rapid strokes.

The whole sordid, wonderful episode had gone far too far already. I knew that with just one word from you I would be in trouble beyond my wildest nightmares. And so, instead of calling a halt to the events accelerating out of my control, and with all rational judgement now completely lost to me, I decided there and then that if my career was to be over because of one gorgeous student who couldn't keep her hands out of her knickers, then I would have to make sure that she got *exactly* what she deserved.

'Stop now,' I ordered through dry lips, and your eyes immediately flashed open with alarm. Your finger remained held tightly within your pussy, however, and your breasts heaved deliciously as you tried to steady your breath.

You looked up at me nervously, perhaps worried that once again you had let me down, but how could you have? The beautiful young woman masturbating before me, just because I'd told her to, was one of the loveliest things I have ever witnessed, yet I was obviously unable to share such knowledge with you.

'Stop it now, girl,' I said again. 'You seem to be enjoying yourself far too much,' I rebuked. 'And do you know what? I think you're just a sex-obsessed little trollop.' You shook your head rapidly from side to side in response, finally sliding your hands away and bringing your legs together, sitting up straight in the chair. 'I'm afraid I don't believe you. Do you know what fellatio is? Have you ever put a penis inside of your mouth? Have you ever sucked an erect cock?'

Again you looked to the floor, only this time rather than shaking your head, you nodded, tentatively and shyly.

'Speak up, girl, for goodness sake!' I snapped, intentionally goading you.

'Yes, sir,' you quickly muttered.

'I thought as much. Well, as part of your punishment I think you should suck my cock too. Is that understood?'

'Well, yes, but…'

'Yes *what*, young lady?'

'Yes *sir*, but…'

'I won't tell you again, young lady. Now sit up straight,' I instructed.

Somewhat awkwardly, trying to make sure you didn't realise what I was doing, I tucked my erection away and refastened my trousers, before standing and moving back around to the front of my desk. Looking down, I smiled to myself with the knowledge that your pretty face was at just the right height.

'All right then, my girl, if you enjoy sex so much you can show me exactly what that mouth of yours can do. It may feel strange – sucking on your headmaster's penis, I mean – but it will be a useful lesson for you to learn. Trust me, it will be an unusual experience for me too, but I am willing to make that sacrifice for the good of one of my students.'

What a deceitful bastard I was. What I was telling you to do was absolutely outrageous and I was well aware of the fact, but there you were, a beautiful young woman left entirely at my mercy. I was abusing my position badly, but it was just too damned tempting not to.

Standing right before you I unfastened the buckle of my belt and drew down the zipper so that my trousers dropped smoothly to the floor. I then slipped my fingers beneath the waistband of my underwear and pulled the elastic wide over my considerable erection, before sliding them down too.

I know it's stupid, but I couldn't help but feel a certain flush of pride as I observed you staring wide-eyed and anxious at my cock, erect and pulsing before your flushed face.

'Suck it,' I ordered, and you glanced up at me, your eyes dark and moist. Calmer now I went on, coaxing, cajoling. 'Look, don't be scared, my dear, I'll help you, I promise,' and gently I forked my fingers through your silky-soft hair, pulling your head closer towards me as I did so.

A sudden shiver ran the length of my spine as I

felt your hot cheek accidentally press against the length of my shaft, but really it was what that cute mouth of yours could do that I was most interested in discovering.

Gripping at your hair more tightly I drew back my hips, before directing forward once more. I watched as you opened your mouth in anticipation, yet not quite wide enough that I wasn't offered the sweet sensation of my swollen head brushing against your lips and stretching them further apart as I entered your moist warmth. I exhaled a deep, shuddering breath through my nostrils as the intense wet heat of your mouth assailed me. It was almost too wonderful to bear, and my cock twitched in response. Drawing a deep, chest-expanding breath, I forced myself to relax; after all, what kind of a disciplinarian would I have been had I allowed myself to ejaculate down your throat right there, right then?

'All right, young lady,' I managed, my voice somewhat strained, 'you've been very naughty, we both know that, and this is the next logical stage of your punishment. Suck my penis like you would for a boyfriend and we'll forget your outrageous behaviour of before. Yes?'

Again I had to stifle a moan as I felt your head nod in compliance, your silken tongue inadvertently teasing me as you offered a muffled, 'Yes, sir,' in response.

Really, I amused myself with the thought, I ought to have also admonished you for talking with your mouth full, but on this occasion I decided to let it pass. 'That's a good girl,' I encouraged instead. 'Now... suck me.'

It was an indescribable bliss to feel your lips close around me so tightly. I watched your cheeks hollow as you used the vacuum of your mouth to suck hard against my shaft, your mouth drawing in saliva so that you might give me the slippery wet blowjob I demanded of you.

Slowly you began to bob your head up and down and I entwined my fingers still deeper into your silky hair. Once or twice you pulled back a little too far so that the airtight seal was suddenly broken, and a delicious wet slurp accompanied the only other sound in the tense atmosphere of my office – my strained breathing.

It was blissful hell trying to stifle my pleasure, and I knew I'd be unable to for very much longer, but I felt it important to maintain for as long as possible the somewhat dubious pretence that I was only making you perform oral sex on me as part of a vital lesson that needed to be learnt. Of course, the reality was entirely different and utterly selfish.

As time slipped by, and you worked with admirable diligence at your set task, you actually appeared to relax a little. In fact, you almost seemed to be using your mouth and tongue on me with the express desire to give me pleasure, and not just because I'd told you to by way of some highly dubious punishment.

Your tongue pressed tightly against the underside of my penis, applying wonderful pressure with every withdrawal and causing my shaft to glisten with your saliva. You simply felt too good and I found myself releasing guttural moans of delight with every buttock-clenching thrill that shot through my body. I couldn't hold back any longer and I began to fuck your mouth while you sucked me, thrusting my hips back and forth, pulling your face onto me, gently at first, but then harder, faster and with greater abandon. Once or twice I heard you choke a little as the tip of my cock nudged the back of your throat, but you were clearly a girl with some experience and you quickly regained your composure, continuing to allow me use your mouth for my own, immense pleasure.

Bolts like lightning shot through me with every thrust of my hips, every long, pulsating withdrawal of your wonderful lips. You certainly had a natural flair for sucking a man's cock, and were far more skilled in your abilities than any young lady of your age had a right to be. Occasionally you would lift your head away, withdrawing my glistening cock from the heavenly haven of your mouth, staring up at me with greedy eyes while licking around its head, before swallowing it again and indulging me with your indecently expert ministrations.

I could feel myself being drawn ever nearer to that inevitable moment. Pulse after spine-tingling pulse fired through me and I gasped and groaned with frustrated pleasure. I actually considered allowing myself to give in and explode within your mouth, or perhaps to withdraw at the last moment to coat your pretty flushed face with my seed. That image alone caused another massive shudder to rip through me, but no, that would have been quite wrong; because I still desperately needed to fuck that tight pussy of yours.

So gripping your head tightly I held you still. I rolled back my head and drew quick, calming breaths before looking down at you again. You stared up at me with those big, questioning eyes, perhaps wondering if at last you were a good girl, if your punishment might finally be over. But smiling at just how delicious you looked with my cock still lodged in your mouth, your moist lips stretched taut halfway along the pulsing shaft, I spoke once more.

'Well then, young lady, I see that you know *exactly* what you're doing, which is a great disappointment to me.' Nothing could have been further from the truth, of course. 'It just goes to prove what a debauched thing you truly are, and I'm afraid your punishment cannot possibly end just yet.'

A tiny moan vibrated against the head of my cock. Whether it was with fear of what was to come, or with pleasure from the knowledge that your punishment was not yet complete, I can only guess, but either way it didn't matter to me in the slightest. I withdrew my erection, watching as a silky thread of your saliva slipped from its tip to fall across your chin.

Leaving your mouth was one of the hardest things I have ever had to do, but it was quite necessary so that we might move on to the next stage of your ordeal.

Quickly straightening my clothing once more, fastening my trousers only loosely around my swollen penis as I hadn't quite finished using it on you just yet, I held out my hands. You reached up and allowed me to carefully guide you to your feet. Glassy eyes stared up at me, and I in turn, smiled kindly back at you.

'You're accepting your punishment admirably so far,' I praised you, 'but it is not over quite yet. You still need to accept what a naughty girl you are. I know that disciplining you in this manner might seem a little... how shall I put it... unorthodox, to you, but it will prove extremely effective, believe me. Now, place your hands on the desk like this...'

I positioned your palms a little more than shoulder width apart on my oak desktop. My hands pressed against the soft flesh of your inner thighs as I guided your legs wide apart, and a little way back so that you were forced to bend forward and to support your weight on arms. I couldn't stop myself from sliding my fingertips up and stroking the tip of a thumb across the succulent flesh of your waxed-smooth pussy, as I stepped away and you gasped and tightened your buttocks in response.

And there you stood, angled over the front of my desk, your shapely legs parted wide, toned muscles straining, and your naked bottom barely concealed beneath that tiny gymslip. You looked as pretty as a peach, but I needed to see more so I reached forward to lift your skirt, leaving it bunched loosely around your waist.

I listened to you release a series of soft, anxious moans, which I assume was a result of the new level of exposure I had subjected you to. I suppose that by now you must have accepted what a tough headmaster I could be, and really, who could blame you for feeling a little nervous?

I stood back, stroking the contour of my frustrated hard-on through my trousers as I contemplated your stunning, youthful body. You were an undiluted vision of sexy loveliness with your juicy pussy, soft and pouting between those smooth thighs and ass cheeks.

And it was at precisely that moment that I finally knew I was going to fuck you, not just dream about it, as I had done for quite some time. Gazing at you bending forward like that I had no real choice in the matter; but still the time was not quite right. You really did need punishing and I was strong-willed enough of a man to set aside my own pleasure so that I might teach you the lesson you clearly needed to learn.

'This may sting a little, my dear,' I announced, 'but it will perhaps make you think twice about playing with yourself during school hours.' And with my last word I brought a palm swinging down against your right buttock. You yelped loudly with the shock of the first contact and I couldn't help but smile as I watched your skin flush a deep, angry crimson.

Again I spanked you, the left buttock this time, and once more you reflexively tightened your muscles and gasped with shock and distress. One cheek after the other, I rained down spank after spank, watching how the blood would surge to the surface and no doubt irritate with a burning intensity.

My God you looked good, tensing and releasing your backside with every stinging smack of my palm. In time I began to temper the cruelness of my spanks with vigorous rubs of my fingertips where my hand had just fallen. It was certainly my intention to soothe you, but I was also well aware that I would be increasing your sense of frustration in another, perhaps more dangerous way.

I really don't recall placing it there, but I soon realised that my free hand was pressing lightly against the silky-smooth flesh of your inner thigh. Slowly I began to draw it higher, brushing the pads of my fingertips in rising circles until, inevitably, they found the soft swell of your wet cunt. With a single finger I began to caress back and forth against your pouting sex lips.

In just the same way that I was offering you the outrageous contrast of biting slaps and gentle caresses, I began to use my words against you similarly, telling you one moment that you were doing well, and that it would all be over soon, before reminding you of what a wanton trollop you were the next.

A second finger joined the first against your pussy, and applying just a touch more pressure it was not long before they were smeared sticky with your cream. I suppose I had known it all along anyway, but your body offered you no way to deny your true desires, and I'm afraid this only encouraged me to spank you all the harder while my fingers pushed their way between your lips and proceeded to lightly fuck your entrance back and forth. You continued to cry out with every searing smack of my palm, yet there was something needful, almost desperate, about your sobs now. I couldn't help but notice how low you were leaning over the desk, and how you were allowing your hips to writhe back and forth quite outrageously.

Finally I stepped away, breathing hard and congratulating myself on the blotchy marks I'd painted on your poor bottom. My fingers glistened with your juices, and I was just about to lewdly suck them clean when a far better idea came to mind.

'You really are too much, girl,' I berated. 'Here I am, trying to teach you a lesson, trying to show you the error of your ways, and I find that even now you are still preoccupied with your own selfish gratification. You are actually enjoying your punishment, look!'

I brought my fingers round to your lips and smeared them against you, coating you in your own fragrant juices. I don't know how I had expected you to respond, but it was certainly not in the way that you did, as quickly you sank your lips around my fingers, sucking them avidly before licking them clean. You were amazing; a sexy girl who was clearly incapable of understanding the difference between right and wrong, and I could see there was really only one way left for me to teach you the consequences of your ways.

'I'm afraid you leave me no other option but to fuck you now,' I announced, and my cock jerked reflexively to the sound of the husky sob you gasped in response. 'If you're going to behave like a little slut – playing with your pussy in public places, and clearly enjoying have your bottom spanked, for example – then it is my duty, as your headmaster, to show you exactly what you'll be letting yourself in for should you decide not to mend your ways.'

Again I drank in the vision of your semi-naked form bent prone across my desk and, my goodness, you looked good enough to eat. No longer willing or able to wait, I quickly unfastened my trousers again and dropped them and my underwear to the floor. Positioning myself right behind you, my legs planted between yours, I cupped each of your ripe, blotchy-red buttocks in my hands and eased them apart.

'Now,' I said in your ear, 'try to relax a little…'

My cock stood just about as hard and as proud as ever it has, a tangible salute to your ability to turn me on. I released one succulent buttock, gripped my eager erection in my fist, and aimed it towards your luscious entrance. Pressing the swollen, scarlet head against the softest folds imaginable, I drew slowly up and down, coating it in your wonderful juices and lubricating myself nicely, before pushing forward from my hips just a little. Your arousal was such that your body accepted me eagerly at first, the heat of your wetness permeating the head of my prick. Soon enough, however, I felt the resistance of your tight channel, yet I pressed on. It was my duty to do so, clearly.

Moving my hands back to the lower curves of your buttocks I once more spread them wide, and the sight of my aching cock finally sinking into your cunt was just about the most incredible thing I have ever seen. For a fleeting moment I wondered if it was not too late to stop, to send you on your way with a final scolding and to pretend that this whole outrageous incident had never occurred. But then, how could I? Not only would I be neglecting my responsibilities as the head of the school, but also, I would be failing to take advantage of your beautiful body and tight, wet cunt.

With a last swallow I thrust my hips forward, stretching your pussy and plunging my engorged shaft deep within. I threw back my head and released a hiss of pure rapture as I felt your body grip me with a searing heat, but any sounds I expelled were matched by the whimpers and sobs you uttered in response to being penetrated so completely.

I held myself utterly still, offering you a moment to compose yourself and for me to luxuriate in the sensations of your throbbing pussy sucking so sweetly against me. But then, slowly, I pulled back, and just as the ridge of my swollen head began to pull at your entrance, just as I was about to leave you, I shunted forward again. I built my rhythm, my cock sliding in and out, harder, deeper and quicker with every stroke. I stared down at the wonderful view before me; the entire length of my cock shining and glossy with your cream, and then a little higher, at that other tiny aperture of yours, and for an instant I wondered if there might be another lesson still to be taught, but no, that would have been a step too far.

I noticed how you were standing on tiptoe now, how you angled your hips to feel me just the way you wanted to, as deep inside you as possible, and it was plain to see that you were not suffering at all through the ordeal of your punishment.

Finally, increasing my pace still further, I released my grip on your behind and moved my hands up around your waist to pull you back against me with every forward thrust of my groin. Your whimpers and moans increased, and you were biting a knuckle, your brow furrowed and your nostrils flaring as I fucked you hard from behind. It was clear you were only moments away from your orgasm. I was close too, as electric shocks of pleasure fired from the base of my spine to the tip of my cock with an intensity that caused me to grit my teeth and release guttural groans from the back of my throat.

It was time for me to bring your lesson to a close and to find selfish release within your wonderful body. Harder and faster I thrust, slamming my hips forward so that my abdomen slapped noisily against your tight little ass. But then you sobbed with dismay as at the very last moment, just as I stood on the very precipice, I withdrew completely, lifted your exhausted body from my trusty old desk, spun you round to face me and pressed your spanked bottom back against it. With one hand I hastily lifted your skirt and nudged your feet apart with a toe of my shoe, pumping my cock in my free fist as I did so. I wanted to see your face, and I wanted you to see mine, and I can still remember the look on yours as you gazed dreamily back at me, your eyes wide and your cheeks flushed as finally I gave in.

'Jesus!' I hissed, as jet after hot, sticky jet of cum erupted and splattered across your thighs, more arcing into the air and coating your naked pussy. I gasped and I moaned, my orgasm refusing to abate, as I continued to milk every last drop from my tender cock.

Eventually I felt my body begin to slow, and with a deep, shuddering sigh, I relaxed completely, my spent penis starting to wilt in my sticky hand.

Utterly drained I collapsed back into the armchair behind me, where the seduction process had all begun. I closed my eyes and the gravity of what I had just allowed to occur came crashing down around me. All too late I wondered exactly how much trouble I had let myself in for. Could I deny it, suggest it was little more than the product of a mischievous young woman's imagination? No, of course I couldn't; that would have been immoral.

It was in that exact same moment, when I had accepted the seriousness and possible ramifications of my actions, that a soft sound once more alerted me to your presence. Tiny sobs and gasps were followed by a few whispered expletives that a good girl really ought not to know. But you weren't a good girl, were you? You were a wonderfully naughty girl, and I looked up to see you still leaning back against my desk, eyes tightly shut, head lolling back and your lips parted as you blatantly and unashamedly teased your delicious pussy right before me.

I watched in wonder as you rubbed your cum-spattered clit with a desperate, yearning need. It truly was a joyous sight to observe, and I actually felt rather proud of you as your fingers worked rapidly up and down. I could tell by your expression, hear by your moans, that you were so close to your own release, and it was nothing less than a sheer delight, even an honour, to sit back and watch you bring yourself off right in front of my eyes.

Suddenly you fell silent, holding yourself utterly rigid for just an instant before, with an anguished cry, your climax exploded within you. You panted, you squealed and you moaned, two fingers held in a 'V' stretching the tender flesh of your pussy one moment, and then rubbing your clit the next.

Inevitably, and somewhat sadly, your orgasm

began to subside. I was speechless. You had shamelessly brought yourself off in front of your headmaster, in his study, against his desk, apparently with no regard for what I might think of you.

And I thought you were wonderful.

As you finally relaxed completely I stood up, pulling up my trousers and settling back down again behind my desk, once more returning to the role of head of the school.

'Well, young lady, I hope you've learnt a valuable lesson here today,' I said, in a firm and collected tone that surprised even me. 'Now tidy yourself up and we'll say no more about the matter, understand?'

Nodding shyly you went on unsteady legs through to my small adjoining washroom. When you were freshened up and your clothes straightened and looking decent again you returned to my office, in front of my desk, staring down at the floor in just the same way as when you had first entered.

'You accepted your punishment well and I can tell that you're a good girl deep down,' I said kindly. 'Now, run along back to class and I don't expect to see you in my office for quite some time to come. Is that understood?'

You muttered some kind of inaudible affirmation before, turning on your heels, you left me to contemplate the inevitable downfall of my career.

Five days later and the school board still hadn't

called to demand my resignation, nor had the authorities arrived to question my abuse of power. In fact, up until that moment when my secretary, Jane, buzzed through on the intercom, I'd heard absolutely nothing further from or about you whatsoever.

But my pulse certainly quickened and a sickening feeling of dread gripped my insides when Jane said your name.

'What... what does she want?' I asked anxiously.

'Well that's the strange thing, headmaster,' Jane said. 'She says she's been naughty again and needs to report herself to you.'

'Ah, w-well, um,' I stammered, trying to gather my thoughts and my composure at this unexpected but not unwelcome development.

'Um, give me five minutes to finish what I'm doing, Jane, and then send her through. Oh, and Jane... you may as well go home early this afternoon; I might be quite some time with the young lady, as I suspect she's been a very naughty girl indeed.'

My Sweet Degradation

The story I'm about to share begins one sunny afternoon in late July when me and my brother were back home from university. Josh had recently graduated and was looking for a fulltime job, whereas I was simply kicking back and sponging off my folks for the summer holidays. On this particular day mum and dad had been invited out to their friends' for dinner, and as it was quite a drive away they'd decided to stay overnight.

Now, despite the fact that I was a twenty-year-old back then and Josh was twenty-two, we had been given strict instructions to behave ourselves and were permitted no more than one friend each to stay. I promptly invited Julie – an old girlfriend from schooldays – and Josh, two of his mates from university. I was mildly peeved that big brother had broken the rules without warning me in advance, especially as mum and dad still saw him as being the 'sensible' one, but when his friends arrived somewhere around three o'clock that Saturday afternoon I must confess, I was rather pleased that he had cheated.

Josh's pals turned out to be extremely handsome young men. They all knew each other from the university rowing club, and both boys had bodies to make a good girl blush.

First off I was introduced to Christian, who was tall, blond and had what American's would call a 'preppy' look about him. It was clear to see that he loved himself a little too much, but as he really was pretty damned gorgeous I was prepared to forgive him his cockiness. Next came Ben with his square-jawed good looks, piercing blue eyes and dark hair, clipper-cut short to the scalp. Ben's greatest weapon was a boyish smile that could be used to devastating effect whenever he chose to use it.

By the way I was dressed you wouldn't have thought I'd made any special effort in honour of our guests, as I was wearing little more than a short denim skirt and a tight, black, sleeveless tee. That said, I do like to make an impression and I'd made sure that I looked pretty damn hot – if I do say so myself – but in a subtle kind of a way.

While waiting for Julie to arrive we all got to know each other a little better over a couple of beers in the garden. As the drinks flowed and inhibitions fell away it was clear to see that I was having some kind of an effect on Josh's friends. Christian was confirming my initial suspicions by proving to be more than a little up himself, what with him being far too happy to regale me with his superior athletic and academic achievements, while making no effort to disguise the fact that his eyes would linger on the naked flesh at the top of my thighs or on the swell of my tits. If I'm honest, I was starting to think Christian was a bit of a dick, but all the same, I couldn't stop myself from enjoying his attentions.

Ben joined in the conversation whenever he could, and he too undressed me with his gaze, but perhaps a little less blatantly than his friend.

The afternoon was scorching hot, the sky a cloudless blue, and it wasn't long before the boys decided to strip out of their shirts. I'm sure they were just showing off, but you couldn't blame them as each had the kind of physique that belonged on the cover of a fitness magazine. As I was wearing a bikini top underneath, I too pulled off my T-shirt, not entirely oblivious to the grin and nudge our guests shared in response.

For some reason the attention I was receiving from his friends seemed to bring out a little grouchiness in Josh, and he kept asking what time Julie would be arriving. It wasn't long before he suggested he take the boys inside for a few frames of pool, knowing full well that I hated the game, but that didn't stop me from tagging along, and I even allowed sleazy Christian to show me how to improve my cue action as he leant over me from behind, pressing his fit body tight against my ass.

The drinking and flirting continued and I made sure that the boys had plenty to see as I bent low over the pool table, before screwing up my shot royally. It's nothing I'm particularly proud of, but I guess I've always been a bit of a tease, and I must admit it did give me a thrill to watch my brother's handsome friends ogling me.

Poor old Josh was playing really badly and getting more and more sullen, when thankfully the doorbell rang. It was Julie, and just as soon as I'd grabbed her a cold one, the introductions were made.

I've known Julie since forever, and fairly quickly I twigged that she wasn't her usual fun-loving self. Josh was hitting on her big style by way of compensation for the attention I was receiving, and despite the fact that I know she's had a massive crush on him since she was no more than nine-years-old, she wasn't even responding to him. So eventually I made our excuses and dragged her up to my bedroom.

Unsurprisingly I soon discovered it was man trouble and that Mark, her boyfriend, had been talking about 'taking a break'. Now, I love Julie dearly, but this put a real dampener on the whole day. I'd been looking forward to flirting and having a little fun with the cute guys, and who knows, maybe even enjoying a drunken snog or two, but all Julie wanted to talk about was how she knew that Mark was wrong for her, but she didn't see how she could possibly live without him. There were even the inevitable tears after a couple more drinks, and I'm afraid I actually began to regret inviting her along.

Later on we ordered pizza and all five of us sat down to watch a movie together. It was just some crappy action flick, but I was enjoying it all the same. About an hour in, however, Julie suddenly leapt to her feet and ran from the room.

I soon found her sobbing her heart out in the bathroom, and resisted the urge to roll my eyes when she sniffed that she was sorry, but one of the actors in the film reminded her of Mark. In the end, when she announced that she should probably not stay the night and would like to head home, I'm only mildly ashamed to confess that I made absolutely no effort to persuade her otherwise.

When I stuck my head around the door to tell Josh that Julie wasn't feeling great and that I was going to walk her home, there was very little in the way of protest and it was plain to see that none of the boys were going to miss her company a great deal either.

By the time I arrived home, an hour or so later, I immediately sensed that the dynamic among the little group had changed, and not for the better. When I'd left they were all charmingly tipsy, but now they'd moved beyond that and were clearly drunk. I, on the other hand, had pretty much sobered up entirely.

We listened to some music in the living room and I hung out for a little while longer, but what had earlier come across as engaging confidence from Christian was now nothing short of unappealing arrogance. Ben too was displaying a side to him that I'd not spotted before, making leery comments about my body that ordinarily I could easily handle, but I thought a little crude given that my brother – his supposed friend – was sat right there with us. Josh had foolishly opened a bottle of whisky, a drink I knew from past experiences he cannot handle, and was steadily getting even grumpier as the night progressed.

It was a muggy evening and the walk to and from Julie's had left me feeling a little sticky, so finally bored of their company, I announced that I was going to go take a shower.

'Great, I'll be up in a minute to soap your, um, back!' Christian beamed, more to his friend than to me.

I just smiled sarcastically and replied, 'Yeah sure… in your dreams,' before turning and leaving to the sound of self-satisfied high-fives and idiotic giggling.

As I stripped off and climbed beneath the stinging jets of water, I couldn't help but think about the boys. I was really beginning to dislike them and it bothered me that Josh considered them to be his friends. But there was no denying they were very good-looking young men, and my mind wandered back to their semi-naked bodies in the back garden earlier.

I soaped myself all over, feeling the tiny goose-bumps that had risen across my arms and how tight my nipples had become as my fingers brushed over them. Slipping a hand between my thighs I began to slowly rub back and forth, gasping and rolling my head back as my slippery caress hit home. Finally I decided it had been a pretty disastrous day all-in-all, and that I deserved a little fun of my own. Christian and Ben may have turned out to be complete assholes, but that didn't stop me from using my imagination to think of their bodies alone.

So, unhooking the showerhead, I brought it down between my thighs and altered the jet so that a soft stream of warm water gushed directly against my clit. It felt really good and I imagined myself left alone with them in the garden, and what they might do to me with a bottle of sun lotion and their wandering fingers, if only I let them.

I was completely lost in my fantasy when all of a sudden a heavy knocking fell against the bathroom door. I jumped with fright, dropping the showerhead in the process, before calling out an angry, 'What?' by way of response, then watched as the door handle began to turn, but thankfully I'd remembered to lock it.

'Um, it's me… Ben,' came the reply.

'I'm having a shower, Ben. What the hell do you want?'

'I… I was just looking for the toilet,' he said.

'It's next door.' As if he didn't know.

'Oh, um thanks,' he offered weakly, before all fell silent once more.

I have no doubt that the stupid boy actually thought I might simply invite him in to join me, and although the idea of his hands lathering my naked body all over was rather appealing, I'm just not that kind of a girl, and all he succeeded in doing was breaking the spell of my erotic daydream. So I quickly rinsed down and dried myself off.

Back in my bedroom I realised that I'd had enough of the drunken fools downstairs for one evening, and so I decided to go to bed. I quickly rifled through my drawers and found a cute little pair of pink shorts and a white cotton vest to slip on.

Now, looking back I suspect that deep down my intentions were never entirely innocent. I've already admitted that I enjoy flirting, and just because you don't like a person doesn't mean it's not fun to tease them a little, so I headed off to say a last goodnight to my brother and his guests.

I soon discovered they were no longer in the living room, however, and hearing the TV blaring away once more I headed back through to the den. As I entered I was greeted by the unmistakable fake grunts and groans of a porn movie in full swing, which very quickly turned into the cheering crowds at a football match as my brother surreptitiously changed channels.

Christian grinned crookedly and offered a lazy wolf-whistle as his eyes crawled drunkenly up and down my barely clothed body.

'What are you watching?' I questioned with fake innocence, well aware of the truth.

'What does it look like, brains?' Josh replied.

I turned to face him and scowled. 'Look, I don't give a shit if you want to watch porn, you know, so you don't have to disguise it on my behalf. Anyway, I just came down to say I'm off to bed.'

'Aw, don't go,' Ben drawled. 'You can watch the movie with me. There's plenty of room on the sofa, right here.' He patted the leather cushion at his side and winked while I simply rolled my eyes in response to his sleaziness.

'Look, if you're going to bed why don't you just fuck off,' Josh snapped, and I spun round to face him once more. It wasn't Josh's fault really; I shouldn't have flirted with his idiot friends, and it must have been very uncomfortable for him to see them leering so blatantly at his sister.

Then out of nowhere, as I stood facing directly away from our guests, I suddenly felt hands grab at my shorts before they were quickly whipped down my thighs to leave me standing naked from the waist down. There were raucous jeers and laughter as I quickly bent to pull them back up, before turning to glare at Christian and Ben. I don't suppose they saw anything more than my bare bum because of how I stood, but all the same, their sheer nerve made me seethe with rage.

'You immature little shits,' I growled. 'How dare you?' But this only made them howl even louder.

'Just go to bed,' Josh said, softer now, but with clear frustration in his voice, and so I strutted out of the room without so much as a 'goodnight'.

As I lay beneath my quilt fury still boiled within me. I had met young men like Christian and Ben many times before; spoilt little rich kids who had been brought up to believe they were God's gift. But it was weird also. Perhaps it was only a remnant of my arousal in the shower, but I sensed a deep yearning somewhere dark and dangerous within my body. It felt really awful to admit it, even to myself, but something about the way one of them had dared to pull down my shorts actually turned me on a little, and I imagined how it might have been if they'd gone further, grabbing and stripping me completely.

My clit began to tingle its desire and I couldn't help but allow a hand to slip down between my thighs.

At first I simply rubbed back and forth against the soft fabric of my shorts, while imagining Christian and Ben getting a good look at my pussy as they ripped them away, but then I slipped my hand within the waistband and began to play a little more directly, picturing them also pulling off my top to reveal my pert tits. Harder and harder I teased, sliding my other hand beneath my vest to rub against a nipple, until the little bud swelled hot and erect.

I continued to wind my body tighter and tighter as tiny gasps escaped the back of my throat. Really it was appalling that the idea of being humiliated by such a pair of arrogant pricks should excite me, but it felt so deliciously naughty at the same time. I could sense my orgasm fast approaching and I moved both hands between my thighs, using the fingers of one to stretch my juicy flesh wide while the other rubbed even harder against my clit.

Moaning loudly I was all set to give in when suddenly a loud thump sounded just beyond my bedroom door, causing me to gasp and hold completely still. Through the pounding of my racing heart I listened intently.

'Will you shut the fuck up? Are you actually trying to wake her?'

It was the unmistakable hiss of Christian's voice out on the landing.

'So which door is it then?' protested a drunken Ben.

'How the fuck should I know? We'll just have to try them all.'

I was astonished that they actually had the nerve to be wandering around my parents' home unaccompanied, but was not yet willing to accept what it was they were so obviously looking for.

Again a crash came from behind the door as one of them must have stumbled in the darkness.

'For fuck's sake…'

And then, in the soft moonlight that streamed through a gap in the curtains, I watched horrified as my door began to open. Part of me wanted to shout at them to get the hell out; part of me wanted to scream for my brother; part of me even wondered if it was not just an innocent mistake and that they were perhaps only looking for somewhere to crash for the night; but mostly I knew the truth of the matter.

But for some bizarre reason I simply closed my eyes and lay back as if asleep, desperately trying to steady my frantic breathing.

'What if Josh wakes up?' Ben whispered.

'Will you be quiet? Anyway, you saw him; he's fucking comatose because of all that whisky. Trust me; that boy's not going to be waking anytime soon. Shit, this must be it!'

Floorboards creaked as footsteps slowly crossed my room. My throat stung dry and I so desperately wanted to swallow, but I dared not in case they could see me in the half-light.

'Oh God, there she is,' hissed Ben. 'Look, maybe we should just go get another drink instead.'

'Stop being such a pussy, will you? We're only gonna take a little look, and besides, you saw what she was like downstairs. Do you really think she'd have walked into the room wearing so little if she hadn't wanted us to checkout her body? She's just a fucking prick tease, that girl.'

Anger flooded my senses. I was desperate to rip into him, but something held me back.

Christian was right in a way; I *was* a tease, but that did not give him the right to enter my bedroom while he thought I was sleeping. Once more I considered shouting at them to get out, even prepared myself to claw at the first face my fingernails made contact with, but I was trapped in a spell and as I felt my quilt slowly lifting away, the cooler air of the bedroom mocking my barely concealed flesh, I disguised a tiny shiver of excitement as a reflexive movement within my slumber.

'See, dickhead? She's fast asleep.'

'Damn, she looks good,' I heard Ben say. I guess it was only because they were drunk, but neither of them was making much of an effort to whisper now, and they would've been crazy to think that if I really was asleep they wouldn't have disturbed me.

'Oh yes, she does,' Christian agreed in a drunken drool. 'Go open the curtains a little wider so we can get a better look.'

Feet padded across the carpeted floor.

'Mmm, checkout that sexy body,' Ben purred as he returned to the bedside, and I felt an icy chill ripple along my spine with the knowledge that they were there, watching me.

'Yeah, she's hot all right, but I wanna see more.' And it was all I could do not to gasp as I felt fingertips pull gently at the inner seam of my shorts.

'Shit, Chris, what the hell are you doing?' Ben gasped.

'Oh do be quiet, you wimp. I just want to get a

little look at her pussy, that's all.'

Slowly I felt the soft cotton between my legs drawn aside, and what I assumed were Christian's knuckles briefly brush against my inner thigh. It was hell trying to remain calm and pretend I was asleep. I still fought the urge to yell at them, but I cannot deny that it felt utterly exhilarating to be so taken advantage of, and I'm afraid I decided to let them continue for just a little longer.

'There you go, take a look at that,' Christian breathed.

'Oh my God, it's beautiful,' gasped Ben.

'I told you it would be. And look, the little slut even waxes. I bet she's had more cock inside her than you or I've had hot dinners,' Christian sneered.

'Fuck, I'd love to touch it,' Ben whispered enthusiastically, and from the idea alone I was forced to gulp, quickly releasing a soft moan as I pretended to shift in my sleep so that a thigh fell that little bit further to the side.

'Well why don't you then?' Christian replied, his arrogant tone pissing me off yet more.

'Don't be stupid; she'll wake up.'

'No she won't. She's had as much to drink as the rest of us and she's fast asleep. Anyway, if you're not gonna touch it then I am.'

I released a tiny whimper from the back of my throat as a finger suddenly made contact with my naked sex lips. For a drunken pig of a man Christian was remarkably gentle, and he stroked lightly up and down, causing my breath to catch and my stomach muscles to tense with every thrill he released within me.

He pressed a little deeper and my lips parted for him all too easily. 'Jesus!' he hissed, as his finger worked back and forth. 'The little whore's soaking wet already. I bet she's dreaming of us fucking her tight cunt right now, mate. Look...' Christian's caress left me and I assumed he was showing off my arousal to his accomplice.

'Here, let me have a go,' Ben muttered, unable to keep the quavering excitement from his voice.

'Sure, but let's make things a little easier, shall we?' A monumental shiver shot the length of my spine as I felt my shorts being pulled down my thighs to leave me utterly exposed. He wasn't careful, he wasn't subtle and it was the moment when I really ought to have put an end to it, but I'm ashamed to confess I really wanted Ben to take his turn at touching me in such an intimate way, and as my shorts were soon left bunched around a single ankle, I faked a sleepy movement once more so that I could part my thighs wider still.

'See Ben, subconsciously she's offering herself to us,' Christian coaxed. 'Right now she's thinking of your fat cock as it slides in and out of her cunt. She wants you to touch it. Go on!'

Now the tip of Ben's finger pressed against my sex, and I could feel his nervous exhilaration as he shakily slid it a little higher to work against my entrance. 'Fuck!' he declared. 'She's so hot,' and taking me quite by surprise he suddenly pushed forward to enter me completely. I drew a short, desperate breath through my nostrils as he penetrated me with his finger, skewering it slightly as it entered. 'You're right, Chris,' he enthused, his disbelieving excitement obvious, 'she's fucking soaking.'

Soon a second finger joined the first and he began to frig me a little deeper, my pussy sucking against him as he drew back and forth. It was all I could do not to cry out from the wonderful sensation alone, but more than that, I was profoundly turned on by how outrageous the entire situation was. I kept thinking back to my brother passed out downstairs while his supposed friends took advantage of his sister, of how much I had learnt to despise Christian and Ben's arrogant attitudes, but also how good it felt to be stripped by them and now, to have my pussy fingered while I was apparently sleeping.

'That's it, Ben, what did I say?' Christian urged. 'Finger-fuck the little bitch harder.'

I could picture Christian's gloating face above me and it both disgusted and thrilled me at the same time. As though encouraged by his friend's words, Ben began to work his fingers a little quicker while pressing a thumb against my clit, and it felt so very, very good.

'Let's get a little look at those lovely tits now, shall we?' Christian suggested, and I felt my vest being tugged up until it was left rolled and bunched beneath my armpits. 'God, check 'em out Ben,' he whispered. 'Like two little strawberries just ripe for the tasting.'

'Shit, Chris, don't,' Ben uttered, but he was too

late and I felt warm wet lips encircle a nipple and the tip of a tongue flick against it. I cried out instinctively, arching my back so that Ben's fingers were forced deeper within my pussy. Each of them held utterly still, but I'm mortified to say that I only muttered softly as though dreaming, and collapsed back down into the softness of my mattress.

'Christ, that was close!' Christian exclaimed, and I could hear by the tone of his voice that he was wearing that conceited smile as he spoke.

'I think we should go now, Chris,' Ben said softly, and he withdrew his fingers from my wet puss.

Sometimes I wonder what I'd have done if Christian had agreed. My body ached for satisfaction and I'm scared that I might well have begged them to continue, but thankfully I was not put in that position.

'You go if you want to, mate,' he scoffed, 'but I'm staying right here. I'm not missing out on this opportunity...'

'Hey, what the fuck are you doing?' Ben suddenly hissed, and I heard the unmistakable sound of a buckle being released followed by the rustle of jeans being drawn down.

'What does it look like I'm doing?' Christian challenged. 'I'm going to make her suck on my cock. Look...'

'Please, Chris!' Ben objected, but Christian only sniggered derisively in response.

The mattress sank a little as I sensed him leaning over me. I could smell him; the musky scent of his prick so close to my face, and I shivered within my feigned sleep once more. As the exposed head of his cock gently pressed against my lips, daubing them with a sticky bead of pre-cum, I released a nervous whimper from the anticipation of what was about to come. I really didn't know how to respond, and I'm not sure what would have given me greater pleasure if he'd tried to force it into my mouth – for me to bite and cause the cocky little shit to scream in agony, not to mention probable permanent damage, or to disgrace myself by allowing him to use my mouth for his own selfish pleasure, but in the end the choice was not mine to make anyway.

'I'm only kidding, dickhead,' he scoffed, lifting away from me as reflexively the tip of my tongue traced across my lips to taste the salty tang where his prick had touched them, and I actually felt a tiny pang of regret. 'Out of the way,' Christian then instructed.

'But why?' Ben asked. 'What are you…?'

'Oh, stop whining, little girl,' Christian mocked his so-called mate. 'I only want to feel her cunt against my cock.' The mattress sank again as I felt his weight shift. My legs were parted without a great deal of care, and I couldn't stop myself from moaning as the head of his prick pressed against me.

'You're right, Ben, she really is a beautiful girl, this one,' he drawled. 'I guess I'm just an old romantic at heart, but I almost feel like kissing her.'

I could feel the warmth of his breath tease so close to my cheek, the smell of beer assailing my nose, and I rolled my head away in response. But not to be put off Christian began to work his cock up and down against my sex, pressing into my clitoris and causing me to open my mouth and gasp involuntarily. And then the supercilious sneak moved the tip of his cock against my entrance and I finally accepted the truth of what was to come...

'Okay, Chris, that's enough, let's go now,' Ben implored.

'Sure,' he mused patronisingly, 'in a minute, mate. Just as soon as I've fucked her.'

Christian then suddenly thrust and I couldn't help myself from crying out as his stiff cock sank deep inside me with just one shunt of his hips. Finally I flashed open my eyes, but Christian simply leered down at me as though aware that I'd been awake all along. He held himself utterly rigid, his challenging stare boring deep into me, and I shivered, with pleasure or revulsion I cannot be sure.

'You like that, don't you?' he whispered, so Ben couldn't hear him. 'You've just been playing with us all along.'

I don't know whether he expected me to nod and beg him to continue, but he certainly won't have planned on what happened next as I reached up to claw my sharp fingernails deep into the vulnerable flesh of his throat, gripping him so tightly.

'Listen, you arrogant little prick,' I hissed.

'You have five seconds to tell that idiot behind you to grab my wrists and to cover my mouth, or I'm going to scratch out your eyes and scream the house down. Do you understand me?' Witnessing the look of real shock in his eyes was a pleasure almost as intense as that of his beautiful cock throbbing deep within me and, his bravado gone if for only a moment, he nodded in silent compliance. 'Good,' I whispered. 'Now do it and then fuck me.' I released my hold to leave him with scarlet wounds he would struggle to explain for several days to come.

'Shit, Chris, she's awake!' Ben exclaimed fearfully, as he peered down at me from over Christian's shoulder.

'No shit, genius,' Christian sneered, twisting his head and once more sounding like his usual supercilious self. 'Grab her wrists and cover her mouth so she can't scream.'

'But...'

'Just fucking do it, all right?'

Ben looked into my eyes and I blinked back at him in the hope that he'd understand all was not as it might seem, but Christian clarified things anyway. 'Look, Ben,' he went on, as though talking to a simpleton, 'I'm going to fuck this little slut whether you like it or not. You can help out and have your turn in a moment, or you can just fuck off and leave us alone.'

Tentatively Ben stepped to the head of the bed and leant forward, and just as he'd been rather forthrightly instructed, he clutched my wrists and lifted them within one hand, resting them above my head on the pillow before closing his free palm over my mouth.

Christian began to thrust, slowly at first, but then quicker and harder. My mind was in a whirl. I was only too aware of how wrong it was for me to allow Christian to use me like this. Really, I disliked the conceited young man intensely, but there was just something so unbelievably powerful about imagining I was being fucked against my will, that I was pinned down and unable to fight back, that set my body alight with a delicious contradiction of self-loathing and pure bliss. I even allowed myself to resist them, squirming my legs and attempting to pull my wrists from Ben's grip, but he was strong and held me easily and securely.

Christian's stiff cock felt incredible as it forged deep inside my puss, and I moaned and breathed rapidly through my nostrils while working my inner muscles against him. Harder and harder he fucked me. Neither his technique nor the size of his cock was anything exceptional, but the kick out of being debased so overwhelmingly was enough to send white-hot thrills shooting to my every extremity.

In time Christian's panting and grunting above me intensified. I could see by the tortured contortions of his beautiful face that he was close and so, desperate to find release for myself, I focussed on my pleasure only.

Of course it was no good; Christian was a selfish bastard in every aspect of his life, and all of a sudden he withdrew and lifted himself above me. I released a muffled cry of protest against Ben's palm, staring wide-eyed as Christian pumped his shaft quickly back and forth in his fist before he cried out and thick spurts of cum began to splash down upon my stomach and breasts.

'Oh, *fuck*,' he moaned, gasping and cursing as he rendered my body little more than a sticky-wet mess. I felt so dirty, lying there beneath him, yet beyond the intense frustration that he'd beaten me to his climax, I simply adored being used like the filthy little slut they'd made me.

Eventually Christian relaxed, and no longer willing to look me in the eye, he climbed from the bed to pull up his jeans.

I caught Ben staring from me to his friend and back again, with a look of real shock in his eyes. He was a fool all right, but perhaps not a completely bad person at heart. As he released his grip on my wrists I gazed up at him, before offering comfort with a whispered, 'It's all right, Ben.'

Christian, on the other hand, had already regained his obnoxious cockiness. 'So, are you going to fuck her then, or what?'

Ben questioned me with his eyes, so with a gentle nod I told him it was what I wanted.

'Um, I... I guess so,' he stammered, pulling off his T-shirt and slipping out of his jeans and boxers. His cock was not yet fully erect, but already it looked rather large. As he stared down at me lying there, naked but for my vest bunched beneath my arms, and my shorts tangled around one ankle, my breasts streaked with his friend's sperm, he began to work his foreskin back and forth in his fist, until his cock stood thick, long and proudly erect, curving outrageously up towards the impressive ridges of his stomach.

'Good man!' Christian declared, slapping Ben on the back. 'I think you should fuck the little whore from behind while I pin her down.'

Again Ben looked towards me, so I gave him a little nod in return.

Christian quickly leant over the bed and rather roughly flipped me onto my front, causing me to grunt as the wind was knocked from my lungs. A hand slapped down against one soft buttock, and I gasped through the sweet thrill of submission and pain as he hissed into my ear, 'Get on your knees,' and unwilling to argue I did just as I'd been told, parting my thighs wide and leaving myself entirely at their mercy.

'Mmm,' he purred. 'Look how cute she is, Ben. I kind of wish you'd gone first now, and then I could have fucked that tight little asshole of hers instead.'

Although I would never have allowed it to happen, the lewd thought alone sent a delicious shiver running throughout my body.

The mattress dipped yet again as Ben knelt behind me. Two hands mauled my vulnerable bottom, parting my cheeks wide, and the swollen head of Ben's cock worked its way between my wet sex lips. As he began to push forward I was immediately grateful that Christian had been the one to take me first, as my pussy was already prepared, wet and yielding, and I couldn't help but whimper a little as Ben's impressive girth began to sink deep. I dug my fingers into my pillow, gritting my teeth and moaning as he forced his way deeper still.

'That's it, Ben, stretch her tight cunt,' Christian gloated triumphantly.

There was no real pain to speak of, but it was definitely as large a penis as I have ever experienced, and things were beginning to feel a little uncomfortable, but just as I thought my body had been pushed to its absolute limit Ben suddenly stabbed with his hips and sent his entire length deep within me. I cried out desperately, my head swimming with colours from the sensation of being filled so completely. Ben held still for an instant and my muscles reflexively clutched around his pulsing shaft, before he slowly began to withdraw. I gasped, secretly fearing he might leave my body completely, but he just shunted forward again and I squealed with tormented delight.

Slowly and carefully he built his rhythm. Over and over his cock slid in and out, harder, deeper and faster with every stroke. Christian crawled up next to me on the bed and I gasped as his fist wound into my hair before he pulled back to wrench my head with it. Through the shame of what they were doing to me, and more importantly, my own humiliating compliance, I shut my eyes to our sordid little world.

'You like that, don't you?' Christian whispered against my ear, mocking me. 'You like my friend's big fat cock fucking you.' I didn't respond, I couldn't bring myself to, but he was right; my whole body felt as though it was on fire such was the intensity of Ben's relentless fucking. 'Say it,' Christian demanded, yanking harder at my hair and causing me to cry out with a heady mix of pain and pleasure.

'Yes,' I gasped eventually. 'Yes, I like it.'

There was no need for me to work myself back against Ben, as I couldn't have taken him any deeper anyway. Besides, the intense thrill in imagining that they were using me against my will was all I really wanted from the experience, and it wasn't long before I felt my body building towards that elusive, wondrous climax.

'You're just a dirty little slut, aren't you?' Christian hissed. 'You wanted our cocks from the very first moment you set eyes on us.' The fingers of Christian's free hand taunted me as they stroked along my dipped back, possessively cupped and kneaded by bottom, and then his index finger dared to press against my exposed rear entrance. I tensed against the rude contact, pleading with a misty-eyed shake of my head, but the unexpected touch only caused my pussy to grip even tighter around Ben's stiff cock, and I'm ashamed to admit that I loved it.

'Say it,' Christian tormented me. 'Tell me you're a dirty little slut or I'll push my finger into your ass.'

Ben increased his pace, fucking me even harder still, and I gasped through my sweet degradation.

'Say it!' Christian hissed again, applying just enough pressure against my tight virgin hole to prise his fingertip inside. 'Say it or it'll be Ben's cock you'll be feeling in there and not just my finger.'

The idea of it horrified and delighted me in equal measure, but I couldn't; that would have been just too much. 'I... oh, *fuck*,' I moaned, feeling something monumental surge within me.

'Tell me!' he growled again, tugging even harder at my hair and wrenching my neck still further back.

It was simply too much for me and I finally surrendered. 'I... oh, I'm just a... I'm just a dirty little slut,' I gasped, saying the crude words he wanted to hear coming from my lips, and as the last one escaped I cried out, my orgasm finally taking control of my body and my senses.

It was so deep, so powerful, that I released anguished sobs of unadulterated bliss, and for what felt like an eternity I was no longer aware of Ben or Christian's presence, and was consumed by selfish pleasure only.

Inevitably my climax entered a gentler phase, and once more I took satisfaction from Ben's rigid cock still buried deep within me, and just then I felt it tense and release as he gave in to his own orgasm. Waves of pure energy radiated throughout my body, causing my arms to quiver and me to slump forward onto my pillows, my bum still up in the air, as softer, warmer thrills washed over me.

Eventually things slowed completely and I

collapsed, utterly exhausted, into the mattress, Ben's still-hard cock forced to leave me, my heart racing wildly. I lay completely still with my head buried within my arms, my poor abused body far too weary to move so much as an inch, and I'm not sure that I have ever felt more alive.

Thankfully neither of the other two dared to speak any more, and all was silent but for the sound of my ragged breathing.

Eventually, as I felt a warm trickle of Ben's cum seep from between my thighs, I rolled over and lifted myself from the bed. Grabbing my robe from the nearby chair and wrapping it tightly around me, I looked first at Ben and then at Christian, but each of them avoided my stare and appeared rather lost.

'I'm going to the bathroom now,' I told them, 'and I don't expect to see either of you when I return.' On shaky legs I walked to the door, and left them sitting in reflective silence.

After a lovely refreshing shower I returned to my room and was pleased to find they'd clearly heeded my words, as they were nowhere to be seen. I was far too tired to try to make any kind of sense of my actions and so, closing the door, I quickly remade the bed with fresh linen and slipped beneath the sheets, falling asleep almost immediately.

The following morning I woke later than usual, feeling pretty well rested, all things considered, and headed down to the kitchen to pour myself a steaming mug of coffee. All was silent throughout the house and there was no one to be seen, until I stepped out through the open French doors onto the sun terrace. There I found a rather worse-for-wear looking Josh, sitting alone at the table, wearing dark shades and nursing a coffee of his own.

Pulling up a chair to join him, I actually felt a little sorry for the poor boy and leant down to offer him a quick peck on the cheek. 'Morning, big brother,' I said cheerily. 'How you feeling today?' All I got in return was a pained grunt and I couldn't stop myself from smirking at his suffering.

I allowed a minute or two to pass in silence, before asking the inevitable question. 'So, where're the two idiots, then?'

'Huh? Oh, I really don't know and I really don't care,' Josh muttered. 'They must have left before we got up, and to be honest, I'll be quite happy if I never see either of them again.' I couldn't help but feel a sense of pride in my brother for finally coming to his senses, and I smiled as I sipped my coffee.

A few minutes later he spoke again. 'Hey, listen sis…' he began, and I looked up to see him sheepishly peering over the rim of his sunglasses. 'About last night… I'm sorry for how they treated you.' An intense, itchy heat flooded my cheeks, but I simply tilted my head and offered him a quizzical smile in response. 'In the den,' he continued. 'They had no right to behave that way and then when they… well, you know. I should have stuck up for you, and if I hadn't been so drunk I would've kicked them out there and then. I'm afraid I must have passed out shortly after that.'

'Hey, it's okay, Josh,' I said, reaching across the table to pat his hand. 'We all make errors of judgement at times, and besides, boys like those two may be huge pains in the arse, but even they have their uses.'

'Really?' Josh questioned, furrowing his brow. 'Like what?'

'Oh, I don't know, but I have the strangest feeling there'll be something those two have got going for them, even if they *are* just a pair of pricks,' I replied, trying to disguise my grin behind another sip of coffee.

Do Not Disturb

Emma swiped the key-card in the lock and turning around, she pushed the door open with her behind. She entered the room backwards, resignedly dragging the cart in her wake. The curtains had not been fully drawn and the room was well lit by the morning sun. As a consequence, Emma didn't bother to reach for the light switch.

Continuing on her way she stepped further into the room, passing by the bathroom and then on into the main sleeping area. With a hiss followed by a soft metallic click, the door swung shut and Emma was left alone – or so she believed.

Emma took a cursory scan of the room in

search of the TV remote control so that she might have one of the music stations playing while she set about her work, but turning towards the bed she suddenly gasped with horror, her hand quickly reaching up to her lips in a vain attempt to stifle her cry. She couldn't believe she'd been so stupid, that she hadn't noticed him before. Admittedly, there had been no *Do Not Disturb* sign hanging from the door handle, but really, she ought to have knocked before entering. But then, this was Emma's ninth room of the morning, so it was perhaps understandable that her concentration was waning a little.

Nervously Emma looked towards the man's face. His head was turned sideways on and his eyes were shut tight. She thanked her luck that he was still sleeping and prepared to sneak back out of the room when something quite inexplicable stopped her in her tracks. It was a tiny thrill that tingled throughout her body and made her feel strangely powerful. You see, Emma had a naughty streak, and it told her to do bad things just because she could, and it began to exert itself now.

She looked back towards the sleeping man. He was certainly handsome, early to mid thirties she would have guessed. His hair was dark, well styled yet inevitably tousled through sleep. His morning stubble was dark across a strong jawline and high cheekbones, and his lips were ever so slightly parted so that Emma could just make out perfectly straight white teeth. Her eyes scanned lower.

The man's chest was naked and lay fully exposed. Emma felt a tiny electrical charge of excitement, and if she had only stopped to question it, she would have realized it meant trouble. He looked good; there was no doubt about that. He was slim and well toned, his muscles subtly sculpted rather than being overly bulky, and Emma nibbled her bottom lip as she watched his torso rise and fall as he slept.

And her gaze slid lower still.

A single cotton sheet lay draped across the man's hips, and her eyes followed the wispy line of dark hair that led down from his naval and beneath the bed linen, to hint at what lay below. She observed the outline of his strong legs, one straight, the other bent at the knee. It really wasn't Emma's fault – she couldn't help herself, it was there for anyone to see – but as her eyes finally fell upon the outline of what looked like a thick, semi-erect cock resting heavily against his thigh, she swallowed breathlessly and stared.

Emma's heart raced and the rational part of her mind was screaming out at her to leave, but unfortunately it was too late for that. Mischievous Emma was in control now, and she knew she just had to take a tiny, little peek.

Creeping to the side of the bed she carefully bent forward. It was almost as though her hand was possessed with a mind of its own as she watched it slowly inch its way towards him, her thumb and forefinger delicately pinching a fold in the sheet in readiness to lift it away.

Emma could smell the heat of the man's naked

body and it caused her pulse to quicken further. It was thick and warm; no cologne, no moisturizer, just a simple clean scent. He must have showered before bed, but he smelled of... well, he smelled like a man and Emma liked it.

Lower still she drew the sheet, exposing the naked flesh of his lower abdomen. She swallowed hard and licked her lips as she followed the defined line where his pelvic muscles led inward in a discernable 'V'.

Emma allowed her imagination to run wild. She wondered if he had enjoyed sex the night before; if he'd hired a call girl – as she knew so many of the guests did – and fucked her hard before sending her on her way five hundred pounds richer.

She wondered if he'd picked up some tart at one of the nearby nightclubs and licked her pussy before calling a cab for her. She felt a tiny pulsating between her thighs as she drew the sheet still further away.

She blinked and released a tiny, involuntary moan from the back of her throat as she finally exposed his thick cock. It was quite beautiful really, all soft and heavy against his thigh, and it was as large as any she had seen before. It looked so wonderfully smooth, a single strong vein running underneath, and she studied its entire length from the base to the swell of its scarlet head.

Emma couldn't stop herself from wondering what it might look like when fully aroused, what it might feel like against her soft palm if only she dared to hold it. She even went on to consider what it might taste like if she was to take it into her mouth, and her body throbbed with a deep yearning…

But unfortunately for poor Emma she didn't get the chance to imagine how it might feel to have this stranger's erect cock slowly push its way between her pussy lips before sliding deep inside her.

Yelping, she let go of the sheet and tried to pull away, but it was no good; the strong hand that closed around her wrist gripped so tightly and escape was quite impossible.

Emma had only been working at the hotel for a matter of weeks, and she certainly had no intention of staying there for very much longer. The job was no more than a necessary evil as she had big plans to go backpacking around Europe, yet needed to earn some serious cash in order to enjoy herself in the manner she felt she deserved. But for all that hotel work was boring, and on occasions rather unpleasant, the money was actually pretty good. And besides, there had always been something of the voyeur about Emma and she rather enjoyed being able to take a secret peek into the bedroom antics of other people – some of them pretty rich and powerful.

Home for the time being was a very chic boutique class hotel. It was the kind of place where the famous and the infamous could carry out their numerous indiscretions in an atmosphere of absolute privacy. The hotel was very sexy, and in keeping with this, so too were the staff. And by way of a reward for their appearance and tact, they were paid a far higher wage than they would be for comparable work at most other establishments.

Upon taking up her position Emma had been issued with her uniform – a couple of rather short black silk skirts, and several tailored, slightly transparent white cotton blouses. At first she had thought about trading her blouses in for the next size up, but as she noticed the other girls with their tight tops and pert breasts proudly jutting out, the old schoolgirl rivalry kicked in and she simply released an extra button to show just a little more cleavage.

Like many young women Emma had a passion, only in her case it was not for expensive handbags or designer shoes. No, Emma simply adored fine lingerie. And on this particular morning she was wearing a beautiful black lace combination she'd spent a fortune on while holidaying in Italy the previous year. It was one of those days when she'd woken feeling rather playful, and as she dressed she would have liked nothing more than to have worn her sheer stockings, a suspender belt and no panties at all, even if no one but her got to know about it. But unfortunately the hotel rules clearly stated that legs had to remain bare during the summer months and so, in the end, she opted for a tiny black lace thong that showed off her toned bottom to perfection, and a pretty matching bra.

Even before starting work Emma could feel her

excitement mounting as she stared at herself in her bedroom mirror, twisting first one way and then the other to admire her curves, and she even toyed with the idea of letting her fingers have a little play, but she was running dangerously late as it was, so she quickly slipped into the rest of her uniform and headed off down to the kitchen for a quick cup of coffee.

Poor Emma tried to pull back but it was no good, she was held fast. Whimpering, she looked down and the man stared back up at her, two cobalt-blue eyes boring into her and a subtle smile playing at the corners of his lips.

'Please, sir, I'm terribly sorry,' she babbled. 'I... I didn't know you were here. I was just going to clean the room when I saw you and... and I was just about to leave and...'

The man's smile broadened further. 'That's not exactly all you were about to do, now is it?' he said with calm amusement, his voice rich and deep.

'I *am* sorry, sir, honest. Please let me go. I don't know what came over me. I'll... I'll go away and come back and clean later. Please,' she pleaded, feeling her cheeks burn scarlet with humiliation and her heart beat wildly within her chest.

'Relax,' the man said soothingly, but his grip remained vice-like around her wrist. 'What's your name?'

She bowed her head meekly. 'It's Emma, sir,' she whispered, peering down at him through long lashes and feeling as though she was back at school, standing before her formidable headmaster.

'Well... *Emma*,' he began, taunting her, 'you have absolutely nothing to worry about...' He looked down to where his slumbering cock lay naked and exposed, and in doing so he tricked Emma into following his gaze. She felt her cheeks flush deeper still, and when she looked up at his face once more that cruel grin had returned.

'Oh please let me go, sir,' she begged. 'Really, I'm very sorry.' Emma jerked her bodyweight backwards, but his hold remained just as firm as ever.

'Of course I'm going to let you go, silly,' he said, 'just as soon as you've been taught a little lesson. You look like a bright girl, Emma. Surely you can understand that you must be punished?' All of a sudden the man swung himself from the bed, spinning Emma around and twisting her arm up painfully behind her back, and with his free hand he grabbed her other wrist and wrenched that back too.

'Ouch!' Emma cried. 'That hurts!'

Ignoring her gasps of pain and indignation he pushed her across the room until her thighs met the edge of the beautiful oak writing table, but he didn't stop there, and his bodyweight continued to bear down on her so she was forced to bend forward from the waist, her arms burning as her breasts pressed down against the desktop, the breath squeezed from her lungs.

Emma felt the man take both her wrists in one strong hand, and try as she might the way he held her meant it was simply too painful for her to resist. With his free hand he reached for the hem of her skirt, dragging it up to leave it gathered uselessly around her waist.

Emma let out a frightened whimper as she felt his fingers grab the waistband of her thong, tearing the soft lace and burning her flesh as he yanked it down across her thighs. 'No, please!' she cried as he kicked her ankles with his bare feet, forcing her legs even wider apart and allowing her ruined underwear to fall down around one ankle.

'Come now, Emma,' he said, his voice calm and authoritative. 'Come now. You must learn to take responsibility for your actions. You behaved in a way in which you had no right to, and now you deserve to be punished.'

A loud crack suddenly shattered the quiet of the room, and Emma squealed with the searing pain that shot through her bottom. She instinctively tried to rise, but his body weight continued to bear down upon her so that resistance was quite impossible. Another slap quickly followed the first, and then another, and the realization that this man, this stranger, was actually spanking her bare backside by way of a punishment was almost as shocking as the stinging pain his palm elicited.

'Ouch! Stop it, please!' Emma cried, and she squirmed on the desk as best she could, but her protests were entirely ignored and he continued to rain slap after slap down upon her poor, burning bottom.

'What's the matter, Emma?' she heard him taunt. 'You think you're too big for a good spanking? Well perhaps you should have thought about that before you started sneaking around where you had no right to be.'

'No, I'm sorry, it's just... ouch! Please,' but Emma's words were utterly useless and she felt her poor cheeks sting with an intensity she had never known.

She gritted her teeth and she furrowed her brow. There was absolutely nothing she could do to lessen the force of his tightly held fingers as they began to smack upward, lifting her cheeks with the force of each strike and causing her body to throb with an itchy heat. Emma found herself tensing the muscles of her backside with every strike, and in a way that forced her to grind her abdomen hard against the table edge.

'I must say, Emma,' the man offered, in far too relaxed a tone, 'you do have just about the prettiest bottom I have ever had the pleasure to spank, and as for that tight pussy of yours...'

'No, please!' she gasped, once more brought back to the full extent of her exposure; the way she'd been forced to bend flat upon the desk, and the way her legs had been unceremoniously parted wide, meant that her tormentor had the perfect view of her naked pussy from above and behind, and the idea that he might have plans beyond her spanking caused her to chew anxiously upon her lower lip and to dig her nails into her palms.

While he continued to spank her beaten, scarlet flesh, she couldn't stop herself from imagining what he might be tempted to do with that big cock of his. She whimpered, her eyes filling with tears, yet in a strange, contradictory way it wasn't only shame, fear and pain that she found herself experiencing. A deep dark throbbing presented itself also, but that was something she was not quite ready to acknowledge – not even to herself.

Emma tensed with every cruel slap of the man's hand, terrified of what was still to come, yet deep down she knew full well that she deserved it. She was forever getting herself into little scrapes and perhaps this time she had truly overstepped the mark.

And then, all of a sudden, the man surprised her once more, yet not in any of the ways she had feared, expected or perhaps even wanted.

'All right, Emma, I think we're done now,' he said, finally bringing the flat of his palm to rest against the burning flesh of her backside. 'You may get up now.' With great care he placed his hands beneath her arms to help her back into a standing position, before stepping away from her.

Emma could not believe her ears. She had been certain that he wouldn't simply let her go once he'd finished spanking her. She'd felt sure that he'd want more. She pulled down her skirt, fussing at the creases with trembling fingers, then wiped her eyes with the back of a hand before turning to face him again.

He had wrapped a bath towel around his waist, but his upper body remained naked. It grated a little, but despite his cruel treatment of her Emma still couldn't help but notice just how good he looked.

She decided to leave her ruined thong behind as it was utterly useless to her now – he could keep it as a memento – so she slipped it from her ankle and dropped it to the carpet. Then she was just about to take hold of her trolley and walk stiffly from the room, hopelessly trying to keep as much dignity as she possibly could, when he spoke again, still calm, self-assured, and authoritative.

'Of course, I'll just have to call down to your manager and report what I caught you doing. It shouldn't take more than a moment, and then you can be on your way.'

Emma felt a second wave of panic wash into her stomach. 'But that's not fair!' she protested, sounding every bit the petulant child. 'You've already punished me! Please don't report me as well. I'll lose my job and I really need it. Please! I'll... I'll do anything!'

The man smiled his arrogant smile. 'Oh no, Emma, you misunderstand me. That spanking was merely a little admonishment for you daring to take a look at a guest's cock. No, there's a much more important matter at stake here. This is an extremely expensive hotel, you know. Your managers can't afford to hire staff who think it's acceptable to invade the privacy of their clients, now can they?' Emma simply bowed her head in shame. 'But that said, I must confess, there's something about you that I like. And you say you'll do *anything*?' he questioned, with a cruel glint in his eye, and Emma nodded forlornly without uttering a word. 'So what exactly *will* you do, Emma?' he asked, his grin widening as he took evident pleasure in the power he wielded.

'I don't know... anything, I suppose,' she replied sheepishly.

'Anything *what*, Emma?' he pressed, his voice sterner now, his face smiling no more. 'Let's not forget that I'm a paying guest here and you're merely a member of staff.'

'Anything... sir.'

'Good girl, that's better. So, how about you suck my cock with that pretty mouth of yours, hm?'

Emma quickly looked up, feeling both shock and shame in equal measure. 'But...' she began.

'No, it's quite all right, I completely understand,' he said, cutting her off with a casual wave of the hand as he reached for the telephone.

'No!' she cried. 'Please don't.'

The man turned to look at her again and raised a questioning eyebrow.

'All right,' she muttered.

'All right what, Emma?'

'All right... sir,' she replied again, louder and with more than a hint of sarcasm in her tone.

The man laughed. 'I like you, Emma. Really I do. You've got spirit. But no, what I meant was… all right, what will you do?'

This time she fixed him with a stare and said in a full, clear voice, making no attempt to hide her disdain. 'Okay, sir, I will suck your cock if you promise not to report me to my manager.'

'Very well, then we have a deal,' he replied with a satisfied smile, even going as far as to offer a tiny bow of his head. 'So, come here.'

Slowly, and without shame, he unwrapped the towel from his waist, allowing it to fall to the floor before stepping forward towards her.

Emma couldn't stop herself from eying his thick cock as it hung loose and heavy between his thighs. It really did look rather large, and she felt her heart race in anticipation of what she was about to do.

Reaching out he took her hands in his, before seating himself on one corner of the foot of the bed. 'Kneel down,' he instructed, and Emma did just as she was told. 'See, you can be a good girl when you want to be. Now, take it in your mouth.'

Emma knelt completely still between his sturdy, parted thighs, staring wide-eyed at his flaccid penis as shame and embarrassment gripped her.

Taking control the man guided one of her hands, turning it palm upward and allowing the full weight of his cock to rest on her wrist and forearm. It felt so hot and so heavy and Emma gasped as she felt his balls tighten against her touch. Slowly and tentatively she leaned down, closer, and parted her lips.

She wrapped her free hand around the base of his still flaccid prick and shut her eyes tightly, her heart set to burst as she lowered herself further and further before finally daring to close her lips about halfway down his shaft. Really she ought to have recoiled in horror as the stranger's cock rested within her mouth, but for some reason she found herself accepting it quite comfortably, almost enjoying its clean, salty taste and the sensation of its tiny heartbeat pulsating ever so lightly against her tongue.

And then she began to suck.

'Oh yes, that's a good girl, Emma. Your mouth feels good. *Very* good. Now, make sure you get me nice and hard.'

As his cock began to stiffen inside her mouth Emma felt her humiliation growing with it. Of course it was utterly outrageous that she should find herself performing oral sex on a complete stranger, but really, she had no other option.

Gripping her fist a little tighter around his steadily swelling prick, she tentatively extended two fingers from the hand that still cupped his balls to gently stroke the soft skin beyond. She drew her head upward, sucking tightly and feeling his thick ridge brush across her lips as she left him completely and a sticky thread of pre-cum dribbled against her chin.

Again she sank down, and again she pleasured him with the warm moist vacuum of her mouth while his cock continued to grow stiffer and fatter and taller. Emma felt it in her grip too, and she was forced to open her palm a little so as to accommodate him further.

'Mmm, I can tell you've done this many times before, my dear girl,' the man taunted. 'I'm starting to wonder if you weren't secretly hoping I would wake up and force you to suck my prick all along.'

Emma had never felt such shame, because in a way he was right; she had been fantasizing about that very thought, but it had been only that, a fantasy, and she certainly hadn't expected it to become reality. So with a fairly flimsy feeling of justification she told herself that she was being coerced into sucking his cock, that she was only doing it out of sufferance so that she might hang on to her job. But her body betrayed her true feelings, and her clit swelled hot and tight as she sank her lips around his long shaft all over again, taking him even deeper within her mouth.

'Emma,' he whispered after a short while, sliding a thumb across the soft flesh of her neck in order to gain her attention. She looked up, her cheeks hollowed as she sucked against him. 'I want to watch you lick it just like you would a lollypop.'

Emma obeyed him completely, and quickly lifting herself away a little she began to take long, lazy laps up the entire length of his cock, fixing him with her stare as she did so. It really was as handsome a prick as she had ever encountered. It was long and rather thick, but thankfully it hadn't grown to the monstrous length she'd feared when she viewed it in a more relaxed state.

She began to work her fist up and down its girth too, drawing the foreskin up and down as she planted moist kisses upon the exposed, scarlet crown.

'Mmm, Emma, you're very good at this,' he purred. 'Now, be a good girl and make me cum.'

Emma sank her mouth down around him with a renewed enthusiasm, slurping away at his saliva-slick cock while her hand pumped quickly up and down. She felt his fingers grab at the opening of her blouse and she almost lost her balance as he pulled her still further onto him, his knuckles pressing into the upper swell of her breasts. Then suddenly the man wrenched his arms apart to rip Emma's blouse wide open, each tiny button bursting its thread to bounce away across the plush, carpeted floor. She cried out with alarm, but quickly accepted the joy in being treated so badly before proceeding to suck him all the more hungrily.

Emma felt his fingers slip beneath the shoulder straps of her bra, and as he began to slide them away she made no effort to stop him. The soft lace cups were quickly pulled down and the cool air-conditioning taunted her naked breasts.

Looking up she watched as he used his tongue to quickly wet the thumb and first two fingers of each hand, before he lowered them to her dimpled areola. She gasped as he began to circle, coating her nipples with saliva and teasing them into two stiff, sensitised peaks. She closed her eyes and tried to concentrate on her work, but it was impossible not to be aware of her poorly neglected pussy and how it ached for attention.

'Jeez…' he gasped, 'that's too fucking good,' and once again he wound his fingers into her hair. It was clear that he was close and Emma felt him press her head down into his groin as he began to push up with his hips. The way that he tugged her hair was a little uncomfortable at first, and there were moments when she feared she might choke, such was the intensity of his thrusts, but at the same time it somehow added to the outrageous thrill in being used for the selfish pleasure of another.

Emma listened, drawing anxious breaths through her nostrils, as he began to moan and gasp with increased intensity.

Then suddenly he relaxed his grip and she was able to lift her head away until her lips encircled only the thick ridge at the head of his shaft. She worked him quickly with her hand, knowing he was about to cum and her pussy throbbed at the mere thought of it.

You see, secretly Emma loved to suck cock, she'd always felt rather guilty about it, but it was the truth nevertheless. It made her feel powerful yet wonderfully dirty at the same time, and in that instant she wanted nothing more than for the handsome stranger before her to ejaculate down her throat. But clearly he had plans of his own as quickly, and rather unexpectedly, he lifted her head away completely. He made a grab for his prick, closing his fist around Emma's and growling through gritted teeth, he forced her to pump him harder still.

And then all of a sudden he held himself utterly rigid, his breath catching at the back of his throat, and Emma stared up at him with wide eyes. She felt his cock twitch and spasm violently beneath her grip a split second before his body released and with a desperate cry, he proceeded to shoot hot, sticky cum all over her chin, her lips and her breasts. He continued pumping with his hand and Emma shut her eyes tight in a vain attempt to hide from of her humiliation, as he effectively masturbated over her.

A few tense moments passed in silence until she dared open her eyes and look up at him again. She watched his chest swell as he drank down deep draughts of air, until finally he opened his eyes as well, to smile back down at her.

'Mmm, Emma, that was amazing,' he exclaimed with a self-satisfied drawl, wiping her semen-streaked chin with the tip of a finger before slipping it between her lips. 'You've paid me back just perfectly, so you can clean yourself up and be on your way now. And you have my word that I'll say nothing but good things about you to your supervisor.'

Emma suddenly felt an overwhelming flood of disappointment now it was all over. She bowed her head, ashamed of her secret desires, and made a grab for her clothes. Then struggling awkwardly to her feet she shuffled away to the bathroom.

Quickly slipping into the shower she soaped

her sticky body clean. The hot jets felt good against her skin and she found herself relaxing a little, but she could not ignore the intense frustration that pulsated between her thighs. She even considered finding release there and then with her fingers, but that would have somehow felt wrong, as all she really wanted was him.

She dried herself off and slipped back into her skirt, pulling on her blouse and holding it together with folded arms, due to it no longer having any buttons. Then going back into the room she found him standing with his back to her. He was wearing a white towelling bathrobe, and was gazing out of the window at the impressive city skyline. Then slowly he turned to acknowledge her presence.

Each of them stared at the other. He smiled, but no longer with devious intent, and Emma just looked away, blushing.

'Will you be checking out today, sir?' she managed, as she fumbled with her blouse and a couple of safety pins extracted from the complementary sewing kit.

'Um, no,' he told her. 'No, not until tomorrow.'

'Oh,' she said, nodding, smiling sheepishly at him. 'And until what time tomorrow morning would sir like to sleep until?' she asked, feeling a strange confidence growing with her every word.

'Well, I haven't really thought about it. I have a late business meeting this evening so I suspect I'll want to sleep until about nine.'

Emma turned away and pushed her cart

towards the door.

'Oh, and sir?' she ventured, opening the door before turning around to face him a final time. 'If a chambermaid was to be naughty enough to try to touch your cock while you were sleeping, do you think you might have to fuck her as a punishment?'

The man smiled. 'Yes, Emma, I think I would have to do that. Don't you?'

'Yes, sir, I think you would.'

Emma turned away once more, pushing her cart out and casually lifting the *Do Not Disturb* sign from the door handle before dropping it into her litter bag. And with a hiss, followed by a soft metallic click, the door swung shut behind her.

A Bad Girl's Revenge

In that single moment I committed one of the stupidest acts of my life, and to this day I have no idea why.

I'm no snitch, but when Miss Barnes threatened to cancel the school dance if no one owned up to writing on the blackboard what actually *was* a very funny poem involving her, the deputy head and a strap-on dildo, for some crazy reason I just blurted out that it had been Julie.

My betrayal earned Julie a week of afterschool detentions and I, the metaphorical death sentence I no doubt deserved.

It wasn't bad enough that I'd grassed-up a fellow student; not at all. It was the fact that I named Julie in particular that was my gravest mistake.

You see, Julie was pretty much a law unto herself around school, and together with her best friends, Michelle and Carly, she made sure that things ran just the way she wanted them to. I wouldn't say that Julie was a bully, particularly – although she certainly had been when younger – but it would be a very brave or very foolish individual who dared to cross that little gang, and clearly, I had been the latter.

Julie, Michelle and Carly's control wasn't exclusively held over the girls at school either. Any boy they had a problem with would soon find himself on the receiving end of six ring-covered fists and would then be forced to live out the rest of his schooldays suffering the ridicule of having been beaten up by a bunch of girls. Not even the teachers were immune to their considerable powers. The female ones they took a dislike to would be mocked and taunted mercilessly until brought to the point of nervous breakdown, whereas the men would be teased and flirted with to such an outrageous degree that they would be forced to leave the girls alone for fear of discovering just how far they might go.

The problem was not only were Julie, Michelle and Carly physically strong, utterly fearless and actually rather intelligent, but they were each exceptionally attractive with it. Any lad beyond a certain age fancied them, and I know for a fact that I wasn't the only girl who found herself feeling rather awkward in their presence. Of course, the girls were utterly out of reach for anyone lowly enough to still be in school, and they would only date older guys with access to money, motorbikes or cars – and even then, just until they'd outlived their usefulness. Salacious rumour had it that any real passion was kept exclusively between the three of them, and the three of them alone.

At the time of my story the girls were going through something of a rock-chick phase, and Julie wore her hair long and bleached peroxide blonde. This, together with her soft pink lips and porcelain-smooth skin, could have given her an appearance of pure Nordic beauty, but she would wear rather severe eye makeup too – contravening school rules in a way that any other girl would have been in hot water for – which gave her a look that was both intimidating and incredibly sexy at the same time. Julie's body was neat, slim and womanly, and she was quite happy to flaunt it whenever it suited her to do so.

As for the other two, Michelle was the tallest and had the physique of a dancer. She was lithe, toned and had a kind of feline grace to her. I recall her hair being coloured two-tone red on black back then, but as she changed it so often I can't be sure.

Carly was a little shorter and you would describe her as being cute, if you didn't know the reality of what she was capable of. Her hair was long, straight and raven's-wing black, cut with a severe fringe that ended just above her neatly plucked eyebrows. Carly was curvy in the best of possible ways – all 'hips n' tits' as the saying goes – and I had witnessed her using her body to devastating effect when bending a male teacher to her will.

So what more can I say? Pretty much all of us in school were either envious of, in love with, or intimidated by the girls at one stage or another, and quite often all three at the same time.

I guess one of the most tortuous aspects of Julie's revenge was that she waited. Several weeks went by with her and the girls doing absolutely nothing. Well, I suppose that's not quite correct; they were actually unnervingly friendly towards me. Each time I ran into them in the schoolyard my heartbeat would quicken and I'd wonder if the moment had finally arrived for me to pay for my stupidity, yet they'd merely smile sweetly and offer me a warm greeting. I guess they were trying to lull me into a false sense of security but, despite the foolish act that had begun my ordeal, I'm not a complete idiot and it just put me even further on edge, making me wish that they'd simply hurry up and get on with whatever it was they had planned for me.

Well, in the end they did just that.

I doubt very much that I would have screamed anyway, but even if I'd wanted to that single, anonymous punch to the stomach knocked the wind from my lungs and I was barely able to catch breath never mind cry out.

It was lunchtime and I was walking along the

corridor that led past the gymnasium with a couple of friends when I spotted Julie, Michelle and Carly hanging out by an old vaulting horse. I guess I should have seen it coming by the casual way they just happened to be there, but there was nothing I could do to avoid them and the fist came so swiftly that I simply doubled up.

Through the din of my racing heart I could just make out one of them saying, 'Keep walking,' to my girlfriends, before I was quickly bundled through two sets of doors and pushed backwards until I slammed hard against a cold brick wall.

As I desperately tried to fill my lungs it was the smell that first alerted me to where we were. It smelled a bit like the girls' gym changing rooms, but beyond the musty dampness of discarded gym clothes and forgotten towels there was a thicker, muskier scent. I looked up through watering eyes and saw we were in a place that in my seven years of secondary school I'd not before been in – it was the boys' changing room!

Julie stood right before me with hands on hips, offering a smile that could have melted the stoniest of hearts. Flanked on either side of her were Michelle and Carly, looking considerably less friendly.

'I... I'm sorry Julie...' I blurted as soon as my lungs would allow it, but I was quickly silenced with a single finger pressed firmly to my lips.

'Hush, little one,' Julie whispered, blinking through long, curled lashes, thick with coal-black mascara. 'It's all gonna be fine.'

Immediately my heart sank further as her

exaggerated calmness only made it all the more menacing, and all the more apparent that I was in real trouble.

'You know,' she continued, slowly stroking a palm across my cheek so that a shiver ran through me, 'you really have put me in an awkward position. I've always liked you. You never got in my way, so why on earth would I get in yours?'

The tips of Julie's fingers then trailed lazily to the nape of my neck and I couldn't help but release an anxious gasp in response.

'Carly's even teased me that I must have a little thing for you, and you know what, she might just be right.' Glancing beyond Julie's shoulder I saw her friend sneer at me.

'The thing is,' Julie went on, as she used both hands to calmly and carefully loosen the knot in my school tie, 'I simply *have* to punish you for telling on me like that. I mean, what would my reputation be like if people were to think that just because they were super cute they could get away with being big old meanies?'

Julie pouted overdramatically, sliding the loosened tie through my collar before stretching it out between her hands. I just stared into her beautiful, almond-shaped eyes, far too terrified to speak.

'The question is; what kind of a punishment does a naughty girl like you deserve?'

I don't suppose Julie's vengeance was totally unplanned, as in that instant both Carly and Michelle stepped closer to take one of my wrists each. Of course I tried to resist, but they were strong girls and they only mocked my pathetic attempts to fight back. In the end they lifted my arms high above my head and pushed them close together. Julie then stepped even closer, the soft swell of her breasts moulding against my own as she reached up and used my tie to bind my wrists to a clothes hook fixed to the wall. The warm, milky scent of Julie's cheek so close to mine filled my nostrils as she worked, and in contrast to the pungent, testosterone-tainted aroma of the boys' changing room, and despite my fearful situation, it offered a bizarre kind of comfort.

But as the girls stepped back, and as I tugged at my bonds, I discovered just how vulnerable they had left me, and it was all I could do to stop the tears of anguish that welled in my eyes from spilling over.

'Please, Julie,' I pleaded. 'I'm sorry. I've no idea what came over me. I thought what you wrote was funny, but... but... please don't hurt me.' I dipped my head and felt my resolve finally give way as the salty tang of tears meandered down to my lips.

I had expected the blows to fall at any moment, but Julie once more spoke in that soft, soothing tone of hers. 'Hey, who said anything about hurting you, little one?' She lifted my chin with thumb and forefinger so that I was forced to meet her gaze.

'Well I... I just thought...' I muttered, but my words were cut short as Julie cupped my face in her hands and carefully wiped away my tears with the tips of her thumbs. I was utterly taken aback by the gentleness of her touch, when all I had expected to suffer was pain, and it left me quite speechless.

'Stop that crying, silly, you're a big girl now,' she chastised with a smile, before her hands slid down to my shoulders, but they didn't stop there and I soon became aware of a gentle tugging at my shirt front. Looking down, I saw Julie's fingers slowly unbuttoning it from top to bottom.

'Um... what are you doing?' I stammered nervously as the last button was released and my crisp white shirt fell open.

'I told you, you need to be punished for telling on me,' she said, almost hypnotically.

'But…' It was then that I felt Julie's fingertips brush across the curve of my naked stomach, and instinctively I tensed my muscles. 'Hey!' I cried when she went on to unfasten my skirt too, drawing down the zipper and then letting go so that it fell silently to the floor. My mind was a whirl. I had fully expected to be beaten or forced to endure some disgusting ordeal by way of retribution, but I couldn't understand why on earth I was being stripped to my underwear.

Julie stepped back and grinned before turning her head towards her friends. 'Yeah, I guess you were right all along, Carly; I really do like,' she purred cryptically.

Then again she focussed her attention on me, speaking as though she were merely teasing a friend. 'Well get a load of you, Little Miss Hottie.'

I only sniffed and awkwardly leant my head to one side to wipe the remnants of my tears against a sleeve, inadvertently staining my shirt with eyeliner in the process.

As I stood there, helpless, tied-up and wearing nothing more than my knee-length school socks, my white cotton knickers and my shirt hanging open to reveal the swell of my breasts within a simple white bra, I was not sure that I had ever felt more humiliated or vulnerable.

'So, just *what* are we going to do with you then?' Julie questioned softly, as she took a confident step back close to me. She held her face so close to mine that I could smell her breath, and I remember being a little taken aback by its fresh sweetness. It reminded me of the blackcurrant flavoured fruit pastilles I would suck as a child, and was nothing at all like the stale cigarette stench I had expected from such a 'bad girl'.

Julie's eyes flickered from mine to my mouth and then back again, and I found myself parting my lips in anticipation of God knows what. But then I gasped, unable to hold back, as I felt Julie's fingertips touch the naked flesh of my inner thigh. Slowly, tantalisingly, she began to stroke higher, and I drew a deep, shivering breath that caused my breasts to briefly press against hers again. No longer entirely in control of my body I felt one leg slide away as Julie's delicate touch drew so close to my cotton panties, and I watched, thoroughly ashamed, as she offered a brief smirk at my surrender.

Just then, and in cruel contrast to the tender caress of a moment before, Julie suddenly grabbed the elastic waistband of my knickers, her fingernails scratching my sensitive flesh as she quickly tugged them down my thighs.

'Hey!' I protested, but it was a waste of my breath and I just stood there with burning cheeks, drawing short, ragged breaths through my nostrils, while she once again stepped back to stand between her friends. Carly and Michelle laughed and pointed at where my panties were now stretched between my knees, but Julie just eyed me with a subtle smile playing at the corners of her lips.

She held up a hand and her friends fell silent again. With a racing pulse I nervously tried to imagine what on earth they might have in store from me next, but Julie just dipped her head and bit playfully on the tip of a finger. 'My, my, you do look pretty like that, don't you, little one,' she teased, and I moved my knees together in a vain attempt to protect my modesty, yet only succeeded in causing my panties to fall down around my ankles. 'So here we find ourselves at the crux of your punishment,' she continued. 'In about twenty minutes' time the bell is going to sound for afternoon lessons. Carly, being the clever girl that she is, has done her research and discovered that the senior rugby team have training first thing this afternoon, and well...'

'Oh no, please!' I begged, as I suddenly understood the implication of her words, the thought of all of those lads finding me in such a vulnerable and shameful state too horrifying to contemplate.

But Julie just went on, ignoring my outburst. 'If you're lucky young Mr Johnson might arrive to find you first, but then again, he does rather have a liking for beautiful young ladies. Doesn't he, Michelle?' she added, raising an accusatory eyebrow and turning her head to peer at her friend. Michelle simply smirked in response.

'And so, perhaps he'll decide to take advantage of that cute little body of yours himself.' Again Julie leant into me so that her cheek brushed lightly against mine, before continuing in a conspiratorial whisper. 'Between you and me, Michelle tells me he has *such* a lovely one…'

Moving her head back a little she then returned to her full, clear voice. 'Otherwise, I wouldn't be surprised if those naughty boys decided to use you all for themselves.' She pressed her hands around my waist and I couldn't help but release a tiny involuntary cry.

'Oh, so you like that, do you?' she questioned, with a sardonic smile. 'You like the idea of all those young men taking advantage of your tight virgin pussy, one after the other?'

'No, I don't, and anyway…' I insisted quietly, while looking down at the floor, 'I'm not a virgin.' It was a ridiculous thing for me to say, and it only caused Michelle and Carly to nudge each other and snigger, but I guess I'd felt as though my pride had been dented and the need to let them know I was just as much a woman as any of them. Truth be known, my sexual experiences at that stage in my life had been limited and clumsy at best.

Julie's hands began to rise higher up my flanks as she spoke again, and I was forced to stifle a gasp from her contact. 'All right then, I'm actually rather impressed that you're not quite the goody-two-shoes we thought you were. I suppose that means your punishment won't be such an ordeal after all, but either way it doesn't matter to us. I do think it might be nicer for the boys if you were unable to know which one of them was there, *fucking* that cute little pussy of yours, though.' Julie's splayed fingers slid across the curve of my breasts, her thumbs circling against the contour of my nipples, where they pressed tightly into the flimsy cotton of my bra and I arched my back, briefly rising up onto my tiptoes. 'That way you won't know who to tell on, and we all know how much you like to tell on people, don't we?'

'No, please...' I pleaded, once more considering the appalling reality of her intentions, but I was clearly only wasting my breath.

Julie's hands left me and she twisted her head to the side, talking to her friends. 'Come on, girls, let's get her facing the other way.'

In an instant Michelle and Carly were at her side, grabbing my semi-naked body and forcing me to turn around. I did try to resist but it was pointless; my feet were tangled up in my knickers and I was no match for the girls' strength.

'Oh please, don't!' I cried, but they only laughed, pushing and pulling at me with increased aggression until I was finally left staring at the wall.

'Now, stretch her thighs nice and wide apart,' Julie instructed, and I heard my panties rip as they were removed without due care. With all this provocation I couldn't help myself, and before I thought about what I was doing I kicked out and felt and heard the heel of my shoe make contact with a shin, quickly followed by the sound of what I think was Carly's voice cursing me angrily. I have no doubt that under any other circumstance this would have led to a swift and merciless beating, but Julie was in charge and that clearly did not feature in her plans. She simply placated whichever girl it had been with the information that the time for their revenge was near, and despite my continued thrashing and squirming and attempted kicking my legs were soon parted, with Carly and Michelle determinedly gripping an ankle apiece.

'Here, tie her to the bench,' Julie said, slightly breathlessly, as she tossed what I could just make out to be an old skipping rope to one girl and a length of bandage from the first aid kit to the other. I suppose I could have continued to struggle, but deep down I knew I was beaten, and so I resisted no more and in a matter of moments I was bound by the ankles with my legs pulled wide apart.

It was an awful experience to be rendered so indefensible, and I strained my ears to make out their movements through sound alone. The gritty scrape of shoes on the tiled floor told me that my three tormentors had stepped away to gather once more behind me. Obviously I considered crying out for help, but the sports block was as good as deserted that lunchtime and I knew that no one would be able to hear me. Besides, the girls would only have then silenced me in their own pitiless way, and having a sweaty gym sock stuffed in my mouth, or something equally unpleasant, was something I had no desire to experience.

All of a sudden I felt the hem of my shirt lifted until it was left bunched around the curve of my waist, my naked bottom exposed for all three to see.

'There we go,' mused Julie, in that overly friendly tone of hers. 'Just look at that cute round bum. I can see the boys are gonna have *so* much fun playing with you, little one.'

Again the gravity of their plans hit home and I tried appealing to Julie's better nature one last time. 'Oh please, Julie, really I'm sorry. It was wrong of me to tell on you like that. Please let me go. I'll never tell again, honest!'

'Oh hush now, silly,' she soothed, and I drew a short sharp breath as I felt the cruelly comforting warmth of two palms pressing against the curve of my naked bum cheeks. Releasing an involuntary whimper I listened to Julie's words, closer again, her warm breath mocking the back of my neck and causing the downy hairs to stand on end. 'I'd have thought you wouldn't mind, you not being a virgin and everything. You have to admit, some of those rugby boys are damn good-looking, and I suspect there must be at least one or two particularly impressive cocks among them for you to enjoy. Just imagine it,' she continued, lowering her voice further until it was little more than a throaty whisper, 'one by one, each of them coming up behind you to sample that sweet young pussy of yours with their big, hard pricks.' With this Julie clawed her fingernails into the flesh of my buttocks and drew my cheeks upward and apart.

'Oh no, Julie... please,' I panted, but she paid no attention.

'Just picture it; you stood here, entirely helpless while the boys gather behind you and laugh in the knowledge that they can fuck you just the way they like, and you'll have absolutely no idea who to blame. Imagine them taking it in turns until your poor little cunt throbs from the abuse and your thighs run sticky with their spunk. I wonder if you'll enjoy some fun for yourself, little one, if you'll be unable to hold back despite the fact that you know it's wrong and you're finally forced to give in to the secret desires of your poorly treated body?'

Suddenly I cried out and threw back my head as I felt Julie's hand slip forward across my hip, my belly, and lower until her fingers curved over the naked flesh of my pussy.

'No,' I protested weakly. 'Please stop doing this to me.'

'Tell me you don't want it,' Julie teased, her

fingers caressing up and down the soft swell of my mound. 'Tell me you don't secretly want to experience all I've described.'

'No, I don't,' I complained, and really I meant it. It was ridiculous. Of course I didn't want to be used by all those young men whilst tied up and powerless to defend myself, but for some horrifying reason my body was reacting to Julie's taunts in a way it had no right to. An intense heat rose not only to my cheeks, but to my breasts too, forcing my nipples to tingle uncomfortably within my bra, and more humiliating still, for my clitoris to pulsate with a deep frustration.

'Liar!' Julie hissed, pressing two fingers into my flesh and carefully rubbing them back and forth on either side of my clit. 'Of course,' she continued, goading me further, 'perhaps your pussy isn't going to be quite enough for some of those lads. 'Isn't it that idiot Greening who's always boasting about how much he likes to fuck girls in the arse? Personally I think he's a bullshitter, and the closest he ever got was wanking off to pictures on the internet, but who knows, maybe now will be his chance? Maybe he'll use his friends' spunk to lubricate that other little hole of yours just before he forces what I hear is a very big dick deep inside you.'

Finally Julie's words were enough to break whatever spell she'd cast over me and I struggled as best I could against my ties, wriggling my hips and protesting noisily so that her hand was forced to leave me, and for a second time that fateful lunchtime my tears began to flow.

Time slipped by in silence and I just dipped my head and sobbed at my wretched state. I have no idea exactly how long I was left that way, but eventually I sensed Julie at my side, and tensing up I felt the backs of her fingers brush so gently across my tear-stained cheek.

'Hey, little one,' she whispered, the mocking coldness in her voice no more than an awful memory. 'It's okay, I'm only teasing.' And with her last word she leant in and pressed her lips to my cheek, halting my tears in an instant with the softest of kisses imaginable. I just stood there, a broken mess of confused emotion, as I drew unsteady breaths through my nose.

'Michelle, untie her legs,' she instructed as she took a step away. Her friend offered a surly protest, but she was quickly silenced once more with a calm yet forceful, 'Just do it, all right.'

The skipping rope was the first to be untied, quickly followed by the bandage, before, with her hands carefully holding my waist, Julie guided me around to face the open room once more.

I felt so ashamed of myself that I didn't dare open my eyes. I hadn't shed a tear in years yet there I stood, snivelling like a child. I could easily have blamed it on the humiliation of being tied up and stripped as good as naked while three girls mocked me, but really, there was more to it than that, and I knew it. Something in the way that my body had responded to Julie's touch left me confused, yearning for more and awash with guilt.

'It's all over, little one,' Julie announced, and eventually I looked up to see her smiling kindly at me. 'That was your punishment, and I'm sorry if we took it a little too far.'

Blinking away the last of my tears I released a short, humourless snort of laughter with the realisation that I'd been tricked so easily. But there was no denying, the sense of relief that my ordeal was over was colossal, although rather strangely, Julie made no move to untie my hands.

'Weeks ago we decided that a mental punishment would be far more effective on a clever girl like you. I do see that old habits die hard where some people are concerned, though,' Julie said, turning her head to scowl in the direction of Carly. 'Just look at what you've done to her stomach! She's gonna have a killer bruise there tomorrow.' Instinctively I strained to look down, but could see nothing beyond the swell of my breasts. 'You are naughty, Carly; I didn't expect you to hit her *that* hard.'

Julie once again turned her attention to me, her eyes deep and dark, her lips soft and gently parted. 'Before we let you go, please allow me to give it a little kiss better.'

'Oh no, Julie, that's quite all right,' I replied, anxious to be untied and out of the changing rooms, but Julie was already squatting down onto her haunches. 'Really, it's not that bad and I'll…'

My rambling words and train of thought were suddenly lost as her hands again held gently the curve of my naked hips. 'Um, it'll... I'll... I'm sure I'll be... um, fine...'

Julie's lips pressed against the tender flesh where her friend's fist had struck me not so long before, the intimate touch of her kiss feeling really good. But she didn't stop there, and she continued to plant tiny moist butterfly kisses in a circle against my wounded tummy.

'Oh... thanks, I think I'll be okay now,' I gasped, but for some reason I was finding it harder and harder to speak and my tongue felt heavy and awkward in my mouth.

'Nonsense, little one,' Julie purred between kisses. 'We've been very bad to you and now you deserve a treat. I can be nice as well as wicked, you know.'

It was then that I noticed Julie's lips moving away from the area that had been assaulted by Carly's fist, and were steadily tracing lower.

'Oh no, Julie... please,' I gasped, as once again I felt the touch of her hand between my thighs. This time she took two fingers and used them to lightly stroke my pussy while her lips trailed lower still. 'Please don't,' I begged weakly, convincing no one, my senses in a whirl. 'I... I'm fine, really.

Julie just gazed up at me through those long lashes. 'Hush now,' she soothed. 'Just relax and I'll give you something special that you'll never forget, I promise.'

It was crazy! I'd be lying if I was to deny having a crush on Julie for just about as long as I could remember, but I'd always assumed it stemmed from envy only. Julie was a very attractive young woman, and so confident within herself that it was hard not to be impressed by her. I'd even kissed girls before, but just my friends and only when we were drunk and showing off. In those situations it felt nice enough, but it wasn't really sexual... not really. Here though, with me tied up and utterly helpless, while Julie's soft lips kissed and caressed so intimately, I found myself secretly wanting what it was she seemed to be offering. I couldn't bring myself to catch Michelle's or Carly's stares, and so I just swallowed once more and shut my eyes tight, allowing my head to fall back against the cold wall.

'Oh,' I whimpered as Julie's lips pushed into the short nest of curls dusting my slit, and then on, to press against the naked swell of my pussy. Her fingers continued to draw back and forth, but with a touch so delicate that I found myself longing for a deeper caress. Tiny kisses drew first down one side and then up along the other, and through my intense shame I allowed my legs to slide still further apart. And it was in that moment that I gave in; releasing soft moans and angling my hips forward in a vain attempt to have Julie tease me more fully.

Suddenly her tongue licked up along the entire length of my slit, the tip flicking ever so lightly across my clit, and I couldn't help but release a shiver in response. Her palms pressed flat against the front of my thighs, before her thumbs pressed into the swollen flesh of my mound, and then drew apart so that my pussy lips were forced to separate with a gentle kiss. Julie then leant in and proceeded to carefully lap at the sensitive flesh beneath.

'Oh, God!' I hissed, as she sought out the swollen bud of my clit, teasing it first one way and then the other. Her touch was so light and so delicate, and utterly wonderful, and it caused me to release high-pitched gasps and to tense my stomach muscles with every tingling thrill she released within me. The way she used her tongue was like nothing I had experienced before, and it introduced me to a whole new world of sensuality, yet at the same time there was still something deeply frustrating in the way she was so damned gentle.

In the end – and I wonder if it's what she wanted all along – when I felt as though I might burst with a contradictory combination of frustration and pure bliss, I was left no option but to beg. 'Oh please, Julie…'

'What is it, little one?' she whispered, before returning to the incessant taunting of my clit, and by the tone of her voice alone I just knew she was smiling. 'What do you want?'

Furrowing my brow I nibbled my lower lip. 'I… I want… I need…' I could barely think straight, my breath continually catching in unison with the ceaseless fluttering of her tongue.

I began to fear that her teasing might simply be a second, crueller phase to the punishment. 'Oh please, Julie,' I whimpered. 'I want… I mean I need,' but really I had no idea what I wanted or needed, and I even felt my eyes begin to fill with tears all over again. Thankfully I was wrong about Julie's intentions, and I soon discovered that she knew exactly what I needed. I squealed through a tight, constricted throat, my every muscle locking, as Julie suddenly sucked my clitoris into her mouth. She simply held me there, drawing back and forth with the vacuum created by her hollowed cheeks, until my legs shook and my wrists began to burn where they were forced to bear the weight of my body. Finally she released me, and with a monumental shudder I relaxed little.

'Jesus,' I hissed, my heart feeling as though it could burst from my chest at any moment.

'Ready for your climax, little one?' she questioned, and I looked down with dreamy eyes to see her planting moist kisses against the swell of my mound, her lips shining glossy with my juices.

So I just closed my eyes once more and sighed a quavering, 'Yes!'

This time I felt Julie work her fingertips against my entrance, and I was further shamed by the degree of my wetness. Any embarrassment was fleeting, however, as the sensation of her fingers as they slowly began to fuck me, shallowly at first, but then a little deeper, took me to a place where the only emotion that mattered was pure, selfish pleasure.

Flicking her tongue against me quickly one moment and then lapping deeply the next, Julie treated me to something incredible, and it was not long before I felt myself being drawn towards that moment of complete surrender – and how I wanted it!

She worked her fingers in and out of my aching cunt for all she was worth, curving them against the contour of my inner wall to seek out my G-spot. 'Oh fuck, oh fuck, oh fuck!' I panted, drawing anxious breaths as my orgasm suddenly swelled forward. 'Oh yes, oh God, oh fuck!' I squealed, feeling my body consumed by a molten tension that surged to my extremities and caused my inner muscles to grip hard around Julie's invading fingers. Then suddenly came that moment of silence, of freefalling, before all hell broke loose and I finally succumbed to the most powerful climax of my life so far.

Crying out with complete and utter abandon, waves of pleasure slammed down across my body, the tension building and releasing, over and over, until I felt that slide towards a calmer phase of bliss.

Julie's expert nurturing of my pussy kept my orgasm pulsating throughout my body for way longer than any I had experienced before, yet even she could not hold off the inevitable, and so she ended in the exact same way as she'd begun; by planting tiny comforting kisses against my wet flesh.

Finally Julie lifted herself away and I drew deep breaths into my lungs in an attempt to calm my racing heart. It was then that the reality of what I had just allowed to happen came crashing down around me. The fact that the most intensely sexual experience of my life had been gifted by another young woman bothered me less than I would have imagined, but it was more that I had surrendered to her so easily, that I had ended up begging her to take me in front of her friends that was so outrageous and damning, and I couldn't quite bring myself to confront it further by opening my eyes.

But after a little time my body began to relax and humiliation was slowly joined by a warm, physical comfort that coursed through my veins. I was grateful to the girls for allowing me a moment in peace to gather my thoughts, and with a last shuddering sigh I felt just about ready to face them.

In that very instant, however, the bell for afternoon lessons suddenly blared noisily throughout the changing rooms and shattered my peace with harsh aggression. I snapped open my eyes with the shock of it all, but that was nothing compared to the horror of discovering that I appeared to be completely alone.

'Very funny, girls, stop messing around now,' I called, with a quavering voice, quickly scanning the ranks of pegs and benches in the hope that they were playing a final trick on me. But Julie, Michelle and Carly were nowhere to be seen, and deep down I knew they'd left me there.

Panic flooded me and I squealed anguished whimpers as I tugged at the tie binding my wrists. But it was useless and I only succeeded in tightening the knot around the clothes hook even further, so as a fear like none I'd known before consumed me, I simply stood there and considered my awful predicament. There I was, my arms tied and secured above my head, my body stripped naked from the waist down and my exposed pussy, flushed pink and glistening with my own juices. I drew a deep breath to try and calm myself, but only discovered just how thick the air hung with the musk of my arousal, and it was at that moment that I heard the first heavy footfalls out in the corridor, quickly followed by the noise of the outer door to the changing rooms bursting open.

Terrified, I wasted my energy one last time in trying to wrench my arms free while listening to a chorus of excited male voices getting closer, and then finally I watched in horror as the inner door swung open and with no other option left to me, I simply shut my eyes and waited for the last phase of Julie's revenge to begin…

Intensive Care

Nurse Libby Simmons was a naughty nurse and I was lucky to be alive.

When I call her a 'naughty nurse' I don't mean it in that clichéd, fishnet stockings and pink PVC uniform sense. No, Nurse Simmons really was a very bad girl, and almost two years ago to this day I became the victim of her own bittersweet form of torture.

I lost three weeks of my life and thankfully I have absolutely no recollection of what they entailed. My memories stretch from childhood right the way up to that sunny morning in June when I was happily riding my beautiful old Triumph to work. I can still picture the linear Roman road stretching far out to the horizon, and the cloudless blue sky above me, but after that I recall nothing until three weeks later when I found myself drifting in and out of an uneasy consciousness in a hospital bed.

When finally I woke fully it was to a pain I hope you only ever need imagine, and the discovery that, among other injuries, I had shattered bones in my arms and legs, cracked several ribs and most frustratingly of all, broken my jaw in two places. It was explained to me that some old fool had pulled out into my path without looking and I hit his front wing at about sixty miles per hour. Consequently, I was in four casts and my jaw was wired shut. But still, I really was a very lucky man.

Those weeks on the ICU passed in a blur of morphine highs and pain-filled lows, until one day the unit sister announced with evident personal satisfaction that I was out of any immediate danger and would be moved to a private room elsewhere in the hospital.

I was still in a crazy amount of pain and completely reliant on the hospital staff, but even so, it felt good to know I was on the road to recovery.

And that evening, at around seven o'clock, I

met my beautiful tormentor for the very first time…

I was watching the TV news, trying to catch up on what had been going on in the world over the last month or so, when the door to my room suddenly burst open and in walked Nurse Simmons, arse first and dragging a small trolley behind her. She turned and stood at the foot of my bed, offering me an angelic smile that showed off perfect white teeth, before picking up my chart and studying it carefully as she bit on the tip of a biro.

Nurse Simmons was any red-blooded straight man's fantasy. Her tight white tunic hugged the contours of her body to show that she was slim, yet had curves just where they counted. I distinctly remember her long golden-blonde hair being tied in a French plat that evening, and the way the thick braid fell across the front of her shoulder until it met with the upper swell of a perfectly formed breast.

As she rattled the pen top between her teeth she stared down at me, and her piercing blue eyes bored deep within my soul. Nurse Simmons was spellbindingly beautiful all right, and beaten up though I still felt myself to be, I couldn't help but be seduced by the vision of her.

All of a sudden she smiled once more before speaking in that breezy, matter-of-fact way of hers. 'Well then, Mr Pearce,' she said, 'you *have* been through the wars, now haven't you?' She blinked her big glossy eyes at me and parted her lips ever so slightly, before stepping around to the side of the bed.

'I'm Libby,' she introduced herself. 'Libby Simmons. And I'll be looking after you,' she went on, holding out a hand towards me.

Unable to speak because of my wired jaw, and incapable of moving my arm so much as an inch, I simply looked from her eyes to her outstretched hand and back again.

'Oh, silly me!' she declared, lifting her fingers to her mouth and giggling like a lovely schoolgirl. 'How stupid am I?' I tried to smile in response, but it was just too painful and so I simply blinked my eyes back at her.

'The good news is,' she continued, 'you're going to be just fine. And the even better news is that you have me to make sure of it.' My heartbeat fluttered at her words. 'First things first, though. You, Mr Pearce, are in need of a bed bath.'

Without further ado Libby leant over me and began to unbutton my pyjama shirt from top to bottom. I couldn't stop myself from staring down the open neck of her tunic. Whether intentionally or by accident, one more press-stud than you would expect was open and I could easily see the golden-brown freckles dotted across her chest, the shadowy cleavage that beckoned, and the mouth-watering swell of those glorious tits. Swallowing awkwardly I forced myself to look away, but she was leaning so low over me that my only alternative was to watch the no less erotic spectacle of her tongue as it played between her teeth. Finally I shut my eyes and forced myself to relax, well aware of what was to come.

Once all my pyjama buttons were released Libby pulled the top apart to expose my naked chest, and then she idly stroked a hand across the flat of my stomach, her fingers reaching for the drawstring at my waist! I was sure I could see a subtle smirk playing at the corner of her lips as she untied the bow and began to slide my pyjama bottoms down. The cool air-conditioning of the room teased the tip my newly exposed cock and I knew that I was as good as naked.

As I've always looked after myself I tend to feel quite proud of my body, and I've never had a problem with stripping off in non-sexual environments. But the way Nurse Simmons' eyes lingered between my thighs, and the way she arched her neatly plucked eyebrows, left me feeling rather exposed and peculiarly awkward.

'Well it's nice to see that at least one part of your body is still in perfect working order, Mr Pearce,' she mused, but before I could test the look in her eye she turned her back on me.

'Right, warm water!' she declared, grabbing a chrome bowl from the trolley and disappearing off into my private bathroom.

As the tap was switched on and water gushed first into the basin and then the bowl, I reminded myself that I was behaving like an idiot and that it was ridiculous of me to think of Nurse Simmons' behaviour as being anything more than her friendly nature paired with hospital protocol.

Returning with a smile, Libby placed the bowl on top of the trolley and dragged it with her to the side of the bed, and I watched as she took a fresh flannel and soaked it in warm water before ringing it out and applying a little soap from a dispenser bottle.

'These days we're told to wear those awful latex gloves for everything,' she began, indicating a box to the side of the bowl, before gazing into my eyes once more. 'But I think they must feel *so* horrible for the patient. I promise not to tell if you don't,' she added with a conspiratorial wink, pressing the soft cloth against my naked chest and proceeding to carefully wash my upper body. 'Mind you, I see by your chart that with that jaw of yours you're not going to be telling anyone anything for a couple of weeks yet. So I guess my darkest secrets will be quite safe with you, Mr Pearce.'

Despite the nagging pain of my fractured ribs, Nurse Simmons' gentle caress felt undeniably good. She separated one hand from the flannel and slowly soaped my naked flesh with her soft palm alone, and I felt my body begin to react in a way it had no right to. I couldn't help myself, and as she leaned over me my eyes again fell to her chest.

Unless I was very much mistaken yet another press-stud had mysteriously come loose to offer an even better view of her firm young breasts, barely contained within a white lace bra.

'You've got a very nice body you know, Mr Pearce,' she complimented as her fingers trailed lazily across my chest. 'Why did you have to go do something so silly as to smash it up, eh?' Of course I couldn't answer, but she was as much talking to herself as she was to me anyway. Time and time again she rinsed the flannel in fresh warm water until my torso was left thoroughly clean.

I then watched as she applied yet more liquid soap, only this time she squirted it directly onto a palm rather than the flannel, before slowly rubbing her hands together. Then with a fleeting mischievous grin she turned from me again and I was forced to gasp a shocked breath as she made direct contact with my penis. It was obvious that I was already semi-hard, and it was sheer hell trying to remain calm as her slippery-soft fingers stroked along my entire length, over and over again.

Eventually a palm slid lower to smear warm suds over my balls, and I felt them tighten in response. Libby's expert caress felt just too damned good and I was forced to give in as I felt my foreskin drawn gently back and forth. She tended to my cock for far longer than was excusable under the guise of a simple bed bath, and through the shame of my now achingly hard erection, I longed for a deeper release. It was hard to tell, with her facing away, but I was certain that I heard her coo appreciatively on more than one occasion, but then all of a sudden she released her grip and turned to face me directly.

'Well, you *are* a naughty boy, Mr Pearce,' she

chastised with a frown, looking from my eyes to my erect cock, and then back again. 'But don't you worry about it,' she added with a deliciously sly smile. 'It's nothing I haven't seen a thousand times before. Although…' she paused and looked back at my standing erection thoughtfully, '…I must admit, it *is* a particularly pretty one.'

Humiliation and frustration flooded my senses in equal measure. I felt like a fool for allowing myself to get so aroused when the poor nurse was only trying to do her duty, but it had all felt so good and a deep yearning throbbed within me, one I'd all but forgotten about for the last God-knows how many weeks.

Quickly washing and rinsing the rest of my body, finally patting me dry with a fresh towel and refastening my pyjamas, Nurse Simmons completed her tasks with nothing less than efficient professionalism, yet my embarrassing erection refused to go down.

Once she had tended to my drips, Libby stood over me and smiled once more. 'It's been lovely meeting you, Mr Pearce, and I just know that we're going to become wonderful friends,' she said unexpectedly. 'Now remember, don't tell anyone about me not wearing those horrible gloves, and I won't mention this…' she pressed a warm palm against the soft cotton of my pyjama bottoms, directly over my stiff cock, before running her fingers along its length. Then turning away she swung her pert little arse out of the room, calling back over her shoulder as she went,

'Sweet dreams, Mr Pearce, and just you make sure they're about me.'

Alone and utterly confused I contemplated my stupidity. I'd thought that I knew women pretty well by that stage of my life, and Nurse Libby Simmons had seemingly gone way beyond flirting, but clearly I'd misread her.

I tried to relax, but sleep would not come easily to me that night, and I was plagued by a frustrated erection that I could do absolutely nothing about.

Throughout the next day I was tended to by a succession of doctors and nurses, but not once did I see Nurse Simmons again. I couldn't shake her from my mind, though. Sure she was beautiful and incredibly sexy, but there was more to it than that. The way she'd played with me the night before, the way she'd given just a little before pulling away, meant that I had already fallen victim to her spell.

Seven o'clock came and seven o'clock went, and at around half-eight, just when I despondently thought that perhaps I wouldn't be seeing her that evening, my door suddenly burst open and there she stood, beaming down at me from the foot of the bed.

'Sorry I'm late, Mr Pearce,' she said, dipping her head and offering me an overly dramatic pout. 'I got terribly caught up on my rounds, but I wanted to save my favourite new patient for last so that I can spend some special time with him.'

I watched a little apprehensively as Libby

twisted a finger round and round a loose strand of hair, before turning and locking the door.

She checked my charts once again and tended to me with perfect professionalism, before clasping her hands together with exaggerated glee and declaring, 'Now, how about a little wash?' I wasn't sure that it was normal to bathe patients every day, but I was in no position to voice any kind of protest, and really I wouldn't have wanted to even if I could.

This time, as she quickly undressed me, Libby leant so low that I could smell the soft, warm scent at her throat. It was a fragrance I knew well; it was simply the smell of a woman, but one I hadn't realised I had missed quite so much until that moment, and it caused my pulse to quicken. She held her face a matter of inches from mine and our eyes locked. She gently parted her lips as though readying herself for a kiss, but of course it never came. Then with a tiny twitch of a smile she lifted herself completely away and quickly whipped down my pyjama bottoms, as far as they would go.

I was immediately relieved to discover that I had managed to hang on to my sense of composure this time, as my soft prick lay heavy against my inner thigh. I expected her to go fill up her bowl and wash me just as she had the night before, but Nurse Simmons surprised me yet again. She suddenly held herself utterly still and announced with barely suppressed excitement, 'Ooh! That's what I was going to tell you…'

Dragging over an uncomfortable-looking stool, Libby sat at the head of the bed. 'Last night after my shift ended, for some reason, and I really couldn't help it, I felt *so* horny. I've no idea why. I had been planning to go straight home to bed, but as I left the building I just knew that I wouldn't be able to relax. So I went round to my boyfriend's place instead.' Foolishly my heart sank at the mention of another man. 'Now, don't tell anyone that I told you this, Mr Pearce – I know I can trust you – but I can get *really* dirty at times and if I feel like having sex I just have to go have it. Do you know what I mean?' I offered no response. 'Yes, of course you do. Anyway, I could tell that he didn't really want to see me and I'm sure he was just planning on getting stoned with that stupid flatmate of his, but I *always* get my own way, Mr Pearce.' Libby narrowed her eyes and grinned to herself. 'So do you know what I did? Oh, silly me; of course you don't. Well, I dragged him up to his bedroom and I just ripped apart my tunic...' At this point she dramatically pulled at her uniform and a good few extra press-studs suddenly popped open to expose a black push-up bra encasing her perfect breasts and irresistible cleavage.

Having demonstrated what she'd done to her boyfriend in the most explicit manner possible she made absolutely no effort to close her tunic again, and merely continued with her tale.

'Anyway, I pulled it all the way open and quickly slipped it off until I stood there in nothing more than my underwear.'

I couldn't help myself from picturing the scene, and inevitably the bits of my body that could react, did react.

'I'm afraid this bit is rather naughty, Mr Pearce, and I think that in a way it was your fault, but I just fell to my knees, unbuttoned his jeans and pulled them down until his cock was released. I'm not even sure that I care for my boyfriend particularly, but just like you, he has *such* a lovely one.'

She gave an adorably scatty little squeal of delight, before going on.

'Please don't think badly of me, Mr Pearce,' she continued, 'but I absolutely love to give head and so I quickly took him in my mouth and sucked away until he was all nice and hard. Now trust me, I *really* know how to make a man happy, and it wasn't long before he was crying out and grabbing my hair, pulling my mouth further onto his cock. Now this bit's really naughty of me, and although I love to swallow, just as I knew he was about to come I lifted my head away and continued to wank him with my hand until he spurted all across my face and my tits. He made a terrible mess, the cheeky sod, but God it felt so *good* to be so *bad*.'

She paused for a moment, looking beautiful as she reflected on what she'd been up to.

'Funnily enough, I felt rather bored of him a moment or so later and so I dashed off back to my place,' she giggled mischievously, 'and of course I just had to have a little play as I lay all alone in my bed. And do you know what I thought about, Mr Pearce?' She bowed her head and offered me a guilty smile. 'Do you know… *who*… I thought about?'

Suddenly Nurse Simmons sat bolt upright. 'Oh, gosh! I'm so sorry, Mr Pearce. Listen to me going on while you're all undressed and waiting for your bed bath.' She then stood and looked down at my body, gasping with feigned shock and bringing a hand up to her lips. 'Naughty Mr Pearce! just look at the state of you!' Needless to say my prick was fully erect and aching for attention because of her story. 'Don't you worry though; as I told you yesterday, it's nothing I haven't seen before.'

Quickly skipping through to the bathroom, Nurse Simmons filled her bowl with warm water and returned to my bedside. She didn't even bother with the flannel this evening and washed me with hands and fingers alone. She took her time with my upper body, taunting me with the slow journey of her ever-descending caress.

Eventually her hands reached down to my swollen prick and she proceeded to soap it up and down. She stroked me even more thoroughly than the evening before, sliding a palm back and forth with a loose grip, and it wasn't long before huge bolts of pleasure began to shoot throughout my body. I knew I wouldn't be able to last for very long, and felt a sense of embarrassment that I may ejaculate so quickly… but it felt so fantastic and I couldn't believe my luck.

'Mmm, Mr Pearce it's so hard,' she gasped with evident delight. Over and over again my prick tensed and released beneath her grip, my chest heaving uncomfortably as I drew short impassioned breaths. I was so close, mere moments from my climax when all of a sudden Nurse Simmons held completely still. She kept a tight grip on my shaft and my cock jerked in her fist. Mentally I begged her to continue, but it was useless.

I stared wide-eyed as she dipped her head and bashfully looked down at me through long lashes. 'I'm so sorry, Mr Pearce, that was wrong of me. I guess I got a little carried away thinking about last night. Will you ever forgive me?'

I would have given anything for the power of speech in that instant, I so wanted to tell her that it was fine, that it was exactly what I wanted too, but all I had to communicate with was the tortured look in my eyes, and clearly that was not enough.

Quickly rinsing and drying me off, Nurse Libby Simmons dressed me again in silence before leaning down and whispering in my ear, 'Thanks for listening, Mr Pearce. I really feel as though I can talk to you. Sleep well.'

Then she gave me a quick peck on a stubbled cheek before breezing from the room to leave me in an even more frustrated state than the night before.

The next day came and the routine checks continued. I didn't have time to be bored, however, as my mind was consumed by images of Nurse Simmons, of the way that one moment she seemed so naively innocent – girlish even –

and yet the next she would betray her true nature as a calculating predator by the look in her eye alone. I couldn't help but picture that shapely young body of hers, those moist pink lips, and all day long I was plagued by a tension I could do nothing to relieve.

When she came again it was even later than the previous evening, somewhere around nine o'clock I'd guess. This time she burst in with the youthful exuberance of a child on Christmas morning, clutching numerous shopping bags. For some reason I clearly recall how, that night, she had chosen to wear her hair in a long golden ponytail, which somehow only added to her look of purity.

'Gosh, I'm really naughty, Mr Pearce,' she beamed. 'I'm on the nightshift tonight and I'm already running late, but it's only because I have great news and I just had to go shopping. Guess what?' she enthused, fixing me with her sparkling gaze and waiting as though I might magically be able to answer her.

I raised my eyebrows and she grinned even wider. 'I'm going on holiday! That idiot boyfriend of mine just surprised me this morning – God, I hope he's not going to propose – but anyway; two weeks on a little Greek island, the day after tomorrow! It was such a pain to sort out cover so late, but I've done it!'

It was hard not to be pleased for her, such was her delight, and I expressed my happiness in the only way I could, by softly blinking my eyes.

Dropping her bags to the floor she locked the

door as before and once again she drew the blind.

'Bath time!' she beamed, and in no time at all she had me stripped as good as naked. Nurse Simmons filled her bowl with warm water exactly as she had done those previous evenings, but just as she was about to begin she suddenly held still and looked across at the door from the corner of her eye, as though double-checking that we'd not be disturbed.

'Hey,' she whispered conspiratorially, the paradox of her sexy innocence making my stomach flip again, 'don't tell, but I've got something I want to show you.'

She went back to her shopping bags and bent forward from the waist, offering me the stunning view of her peach-like bottom encased within that tight white tunic.

'Ta-daaa!' she suddenly squealed delightfully, spinning around and clutching a tiny striped bikini. 'It's for my holiday. I just had to buy it.' Libby furrowed her brow a little before continuing, 'Although, those big meanies at the shop wouldn't let me try it on.' Suddenly her eyes grew wide and a cheeky smile spread across her lips. 'I know!' she exclaimed. 'You wouldn't mind if I tried it properly now, would you?'

Libby didn't even wait for me to shake my head; she simply turned to face away and peeled apart the front of her uniform. 'No peaking now, Mr Pearce,' she teased, but I suspect that she had no problem whatsoever with me watching her change.

Nurse Simmons let her tunic slide from her

shoulders to the floor in one tantalising shimmer, to reveal the crème-caramel flesh of her rear. Her body was as toned and just as well sculpted as I had imagined it to be, and I was stricken with a rapidly growing erection yet again.

She was wearing plain underwear, black cotton with lycra, but its simplicity did nothing to spoil the seductive image of her near-naked state. Quickly reaching behind her back she unclipped the bra and tossed it aside. Next she slipped off her panties to reveal the perfectly round curve of her bottom. In no time at all she'd smoothed on the new bikini and spinning around, she beamed at me excitedly.

'So? What do you think?'

What did I think? I thought she looked incredible, but of course I had no way to vocalise it. Libby playfully offered me a few over-the-top glamour model poses, and allowed me to take in the wonderful spectacle of her body more fully. Her bikini bottoms were tiny, tying in two bows at the hips, and exposed the gentle curve of a tummy, that I have always found to be incredibly erotic on a woman. Yes, Libby Simmons looked good enough to eat, and I could do absolutely nothing about it.

'*You* need a shave, Mr Pearce,' she suddenly announced, and it was all a little surreal to be tended to by a beauty in a bikini, and I could almost imagine myself in one of those ridiculous hip-hop videos as Libby lathered my face with an old fashioned soap and brush before proceeding to treat me to a wet shave. She was very careful and highly attentive, and I watched as she set about her task, the tip of her tongue poking between her lips as she concentrated.

Occasionally our eyes would meet and she would offer me a naughty grin, but always she would return to her duties with the steady precision of a master surgeon.

Once done she rinsed off my face and towel-patted it dry before running the tips of her fingers across my cheek. 'Ooh, that's much better, Mr Pearce. You're all smooth and lovely now. So, anywhere else you want shaving?' she teased, raising her eyebrows before looking down towards my stiff prick. '*Mister* Pearce!' she chastised. 'You really are a very naughty boy, aren't you? But I suppose I can't blame you; I do look amazing in this bikini, don't I? Hey! We need some fresh water.'

She skipped off to the bathroom again and turned the tap on, calling back to me as she filled the bowl. 'You know, Mr Pearce, I have no idea why I even bought this bikini top anyway. I've got no intention of wearing it.'

I didn't notice at first, what with the way she held the metal bowl before her as she returned to my bedside, but Libby's cheeky smile let me know she was up to something, and as she leant over to set the bowl down I was immediately taken aback to see that she was now topless, and quite proudly displaying her superb tits to me. Nurse Simmons straightened up and stood with feet neatly together and hands clasped behind her back, swinging her hips coquettishly from side-to-side as I eyed her lush pink nipples.

'What do you think?' she asked, playing it all coy. 'I must confess I do love my boobs, Mr Pearce. I know they're not the biggest or anything, but "more than a handful's a waste", as they say, and besides, I simply adore the way they feel when played with.' With this Libby lifted her hands, cupped those gorgeous breasts, and began to tease each nipple with her thumbs.

'Mmm,' she purred, briefly shutting her eyes and wrinkling her lovely little nose, before staring at me once more and smiling naughtily. 'I hope you don't think I'm *too* rude, Mr Pearce, but I do feel very comfortable with you, you know, and I figure if all those men on the beach will get to see me like this then there's no harm if you do too. But anyway, silly me, carrying on away when you must be getting all chilly.'

Nurse Simmons proceeded to bathe me just as before from shoulders down, but this time I had the added torture of being able to stare at her naked breasts as she worked. I could see how the tip of each rosy-red nipple had stiffened a little from her teasing, and I couldn't stop myself from wondering how they might feel between my lips, how they'd taste.

Libby's hands slipped lower across my body, and this time I was determined to find release. I was already wound as tight as a drum and I was certain that with just the lightest caress I'd be unable to resist, but once again mischievous Nurse Simmons had plans of her own. With one hand she gently soaped my balls and the sensitive flesh around my groin, and with the other she tightly gripped the girth of my shaft. I watched as she bent low over me, a delightful look of concentration on her lovely face, and a sudden shiver rippled along my spine in unison with the warm caress of her breath as it drifted against the exposed tip of my cock. She was so close to touching me with her lips, and despite the discomfort of my aching body I tensed my buttocks and tried in vain to thrust myself closer towards her.

'Gosh, it really is a pretty one you know,' she sighed softly. 'Forgive me, Mr Pearce, but I've started to wonder how it might feel in my mouth. Or even… in my…' Her voice trailed off, and as though a switch had suddenly been flicked in her mind she lifted away and proceeded to rinse, dry and dress me with formal efficiency.

Nurse Simmons then checked my charts and made tiny adjustments to the equipment that surrounded me, before quickly slipping back into her tunic without even bothering to change back into her underwear. At the last moment, just as she unlocked and opened the door, she turned, smiled and blew me a kiss before leaving as quickly as she had entered.

This time I was left in no doubt that I was little more than a plaything in her cruel, tormenting game. No one could be that naive, and I felt an anger surge within me that was only surpassed by my extreme sexual frustration.

The following day I found myself both dreading and longing for Libby's next visit. It was ridiculous; I knew she was using me, but some small part of me still prayed that in the end Nurse Simmons would become too involved in her own selfish pleasure to stop me from taking my own.

At around eight-thirty that evening my door opened and I looked up expectantly, only to see one of the older nurses cheerily bustling into my room. I don't mind admitting that I was deeply disappointed when she set about the usual tasks that Libby would have tended to, and I was even given a quick bed bath, but it was nowhere near as intimate or as sexy an experience as it was with Nurse Simmons, which was a blessing, because as lovely though this nurse was, she was not exactly my type. I was awkwardly changed into fresh pyjamas before being left alone for the evening.

In my solitude I wondered if I had perhaps misheard Libby, and that she had already left for her holiday, and foolishly I even felt a little affronted by her not bothering to say goodbye to me.

But some time after ten o'clock I was just drifting off to sleep when I became aware of a soft tapping at my door, as it slowly opened. I almost didn't recognise her in the soft glow of my reading light, but then she spoke and all became clear. 'Are you awake, Mr Pearce?' Libby was not dressed in her uniform, and her blonde hair fell loose in soft waves to her shoulders. She was wearing a subtle pale-yellow flower-print dress, which followed the flow of her curves just perfectly. I had never seen her looking more stunning, but I was still annoyed with her and it must have shown in my expression.

'Hey, are you okay?' she softly called, apparently with genuine concern. 'You don't look your usual self.'

Libby came in and close the door, then picked up my chart from the foot of the bed and hurriedly scanned through the most recent entries. 'All looks good here,' she declared with a frown, quickly stepping to the side of the bed and laying a cool palm against my forehead. 'Well your temperature seems fine too. So what's the matter?'

Clearly I was still incapable of answering, and even if I had been there was still a small part of me that wondered if I was not just imagining that she was purposefully taunting me, that her intentions were not essentially innocent.

'Is it because I wasn't here to look after you tonight?' she suggested with a pout. 'Oh, my poor Mr Pearce. You're still my favourite patient, you know. I promise. They just made me go work on the antenatal ward as someone had gone off sick, but I'm here for you now. Did you really think I'd go on holiday without saying goodbye to my Mr Pearce?' Libby quickly leant down and pressed her lips against my ear. 'Silly you,' she whispered. 'And besides, I've got something rather special I want to show you.'

As she straightened up again Nurse Simmons coyly looked down at me with those big blue eyes, and I knew I was in trouble.

'I did something today, Mr Pearce,' she announced, stepping back from the bed so I could get a better look at her. 'I had a professional wax in readiness for my holiday. Don't my legs look pretty?' Quickly she spun round, causing her dress to flair out and show off her gorgeously shapely legs, before she stopped and smiled at me once more.

'But that's not all, Mr Pearce,' she whispered conspiratorially. 'I had somewhere else waxed too,' and without a further word she lifted her dress until her silky-smooth thighs were exposed more fully again. But she didn't stop there. Nurse Simmons continued to raise her hands until she revealed her neat pussy, all naked and waxed completely bare.

'Oh Mr Pearce, don't think badly of me for not wearing any knickers today, will you?' she uttered quickly. 'I had my wax this morning and it just felt too nice to have the breeze tease beneath my uniform, and when I got changed into my dress I simply couldn't bear to wear panties too.'

I stared between her thighs, swallowing awkwardly as she parted her legs just a little wider. 'It feels *so* soft, Mr Pearce, just like a little kitten,' and she allowed the tips of two fingers to press against the swell of her mound and to stroke up and down. 'And I'm afraid… I've been quite unable to stop myself from playing with it a few times already today.' My stiff cock throbbed with the dissatisfaction of its neglect within my pyjamas. 'I so wish you could feel how smooth it is too, Mr Pearce.' Libby shut her eyes and allowed her fingertips to continue their caresses, and I was powerless not to stare at her sexy display. 'But with your arms in those stupid casts and everything...'

Suddenly her eyes snapped open, her fingers holding completely still. 'Unless...' she looked down at me with a devilish grin. 'Oh, you have to feel it, Mr Pearce. I know you'll just love it as well.'

Quickly Nurse Libby locked the door to my room, slipped off her shoes and was at the side of my bed, pulling down my pyjama bottoms. 'Mmm, lovely,' she purred, shooting me a sideways glance. I watched aghast as she clambered up onto the bed and carefully straddled my thighs, facing towards me, before once again she lifted her dress. I could see her pussy more clearly now and it really was a thing of beauty; smooth and flushed pink with arousal.

'Now,' she whispered as she dipped her face towards me, 'tell me that you've ever felt anything softer and I won't believe you.' Taking my erect shaft within a cool fist she pulled it back a little before lowering herself so that the scarlet head touched against the swell of her cunt lips. Gently moving on her knees Libby began to draw me against her waxed flesh. She shut her eyes and parted her sexy, moist lips, gasping and teasing her milky-white teeth with the tip of her tongue.

'Oh!' she cried softly. 'What do you... um,

what do you think?' But she was paying absolutely no attention to my thoughts as she began to rub me against herself more eagerly.

Nurse Simmons rose up and then down, rubbing the tip of my cock against her clit. She drew it first one way and then the other, moaning and crying out with every thrill she elicited. Soon enough, and quite naturally, I felt Libby begin to work me against her slit. Her lips parted for me and she stroked back and forth until the wet warmth of her cream began to smear against the tip of my prick.

'Oh... oh God, Mr Pearce,' she moaned, her eyes held tightly shut as she directed me to her entrance. At long last she was going to fuck me, and the anticipation was a torture of the sweetest kind. Tentatively she bore down and I felt the resistance of her juicy flesh press against me. Two or three times more she lifted away to reposition herself, until finally her body yielded and the head of my cock began to enter her. I couldn't help but release a guttural moan from the back of my throat and Libby hissed with her own delight. As she held me at her entrance I tried to raise my hips to meet her, but it was simply too damned awkward and so I waited for her to sink down on me entirely.

But Libby merely lifted herself away once more, and just as I was about to leave her body entirely she dropped down again, but exactly as before, so that only the head of my cock was allowed to slip inside.

'Oh, Mr Pearce!' she exclaimed with a breathy

cry, opening her eyes and pouting down at me. 'That feels just too good. God, I wish we could just do it.' I desperately tried to tell her through my stare that it was all right, that she was welcome to take advantage of my body, but as usual she seemed to miss my desperate signals.

'Oh, you feel so nice and I really want all of that lovely cock of yours to fill me deep inside, but it would be wrong of me to take advantage of a patient in that way. I could lose my job, and... oh!'

I strained to look and saw that she was now rubbing her clit with two fingers, while the tip of my prick remained held at her entrance.

'Oh fuck...' she squealed. 'Oh... Mr Pearce,' she gasped, and it was plain to see by the tortured furrowing of her lightly perspiring brow that she was nearing her climax, and then Nurse Simmons fell silent, her beautiful breasts heaving and her mouth slightly open as she gave in, crying out and falling forward to support herself on one arm above me. 'Oh, Jesus!' she exclaimed, her eyes remaining closed. 'That was... you are... oh fuck!'

Eventually her body relaxed and she lifted herself away from my still rigid cock. Looking down at me, her eyes dreamy and pupils dilated, she offered me a shy smile. 'God, I'm so sorry Mr Pearce. I... I don't know what came over me. I just couldn't help myself. What must you think of me?'

It was, of course, a rhetorical question, but really I didn't know the answer anyway. I had never desired, never wanted anyone so completely, but it would not be too strong a word to say that I was beginning to hate her for the tormenting hell she was subjecting me to. But Nurse Simmons wasn't quite done with me yet...

Rising high on her knees and arching her back, Libby forked her fingers through her thick mane of hair and sighed. She lifted her skirt a little way and stared down at my still stiff prick beneath her. 'Oh gosh, look what I've done to your penis,' she said cheekily. 'It's all sticky, and you were so nice and clean when I got here. I know...' Libby quickly and with amazing agility swapped her legs over so that she now straddled my torso in the opposite direction, facing away from me. Again a soft hand gripped tight at the base of my shaft, directing it back a little, and I was powerless not to groan as she dipped down and her moist lips suddenly closed around the head of my cock. Then Libby's next move made it obvious that she had known exactly what she was doing all along, as her free hand reached back to lift her dress until it lay bunched around her waist, her delicious cunt exposed to me again. Seemingly determined to show me still more she gripped a naked buttock and pulled it away from its lovely twin, and I couldn't help but stare at her tight young pussy, all rosy from her orgasm.

I wanted to fuck her with my fingers as she sucked on my cock, I wanted to lap at her clit and to tease her arsehole with the tip of a thumb, but clearly I was incapable of doing anything of the sort. But one thing I could experience clearly was her musky scent, and it caused my prick to spasm in her mouth. Her tongue flicked against me as she licked her own sticky juices. My dick twitched and jerked within her grip and I considered what a wonderful revenge it would be to shoot all across that pretty face of hers, but as always Nurse Libby Simmons was one step ahead, and before I could reach my orgasm she lifted herself upright and gracefully slipped from the bed.

She pulled up my pyjama bottoms with the careful professionalism of one who had done so a thousand times, and I found myself wondering just how many other men had fallen victim to her game. Libby smiled down at me with a look of angelic innocence.

'Gosh I'm going to miss you, Mr Pearce,' she whispered huskily, leaning down and kissing me lightly on the lips, my torment continuing as her lovely breasts pressed softly against my chest. 'Just you make sure that you keep on getting better while I'm away, you hear?' She blinked cutely at me and caressed my cheek with a thumb, before straightening up, turning and calmly walking to the door, and just before she opened it she turned to face me once more.

'Oh, and Mr Pearce, when I allow my boyfriend to fuck me on the beach tomorrow night, it'll be you I'll be thinking of and not him.'

And then she left, and all I could do was stare at the closed door. Nurse Simmons had beaten me yet again, and I'm not afraid to say that this time I was glad to see her gone.

Wonderful things began to happen to me over the next two weeks. There were still tests, x-rays and scans to be endured, but the first piece of good news arrived one morning when I was told that my arm-casts were to be removed. I ached like hell and my muscles had wasted more than a little, but it was a life changing experience nevertheless. Finally I could drag myself from bed to wheelchair all by myself, and most importantly, go unaccompanied to the bathroom. And yes, almost the second that I was left alone I unleashed the sexual tension that had plagued me from the very first moment that Nurse Simmons walked into my life. By way of a pathetic revenge I tried my hardest not to think of her, but of course I couldn't help myself. In the end I was glad that I did though, as it was during those first brief pleasure-filled moments that my plan began to formulate.

The physiotherapy sessions began in earnest, and then first one leg cast was removed, quickly followed by the other a couple of days later. I felt as weak and as ungainly as a newborn foal, but my sense of elation at being able to walk again, when things could so easily have ended much more seriously, was unparalleled.

There have to be easier ways to get in shape, but as I stepped from the shower one evening – a shower I'd joyously been able to give myself – I caught my reflection in the mirror and realised that I actually looked rather good. The high protein liquid diet I was forced to endure because of my broken jaw had given me all the nutrients I could possibly need, but my body had naturally shed a few excess pounds in the process, and I looked leaner and more defined than at any time over the last few years.

So with a new lease of life I threw myself into getting fit, and one morning, while undertaking a set of squats in my room, I spotted a so far undiscovered feature of my hospital bed. In each corner a soft leather strap hung down beneath the mattress. There appeared to be a velcro fastener at one end, and upon closer inspection I quickly worked out what they were for. By pulling them along the chrome tubing of the bedrails and up above the mattress it was plain to see that they were restraints of some sort. I don't suppose that they were for aggressive patients or for those inclined to self-harm, as they didn't quite look secure enough, but as I closed a loop around my wrist I discovered that you would really have to fight pretty hard to break free. I suspect they were for those in danger of moving damaged limbs in their sleep, or perhaps patients who suffered from fits.

Either way they were an interesting discovery, and as I tucked them back out of view I smiled to myself.

Ten days after Libby left for her holiday the best development of all occurred. My jaw was finally unwired. After weeks without use, so much as opening my mouth even a fraction resulted in a dull, throbbing pain, but I was ecstatic nonetheless. My tongue felt as though it didn't belong in my mouth, and talking was both weird and wonderful at the same time. But the food... even bland, unexciting hospital food tasted like the finest Michelin Star cuisine.

I had half expected to be discharged, but the consultant explained to me one morning that there was still a little internal bruising they would like to keep an eye on for a day or two, and that I would be better off being close at hand for the twice-daily physiotherapy sessions anyway. I was truly sick of the hospital, but as I was single I had nowhere to be in a hurry, and so I used what time I had left to enjoy walks in the sunshine in the hospital grounds, talking to anyone who would listen, and eating and drinking as though for the very first time in my life. But of course, one part of my mind was always fixed on something else, or perhaps I should say, *someone* else.

The inevitable day arrived. I won't say that it crept up on me, or that I'd lost track, as that would be a lie. I'd been mentally ticking off each twenty-four hours, one after the other, and had even made an effort to charm the ward sister into divulging when Nurse Simmons would be returning to work.

The fateful evening was a balmy one, and so I lay on my bed in nothing more than a fresh pair of pyjama bottoms, reading a rather poor detective novel I had borrowed from a new friend in my physio class. What little breeze there was teased its way through the open window. It was not quite dark yet, but the room was dull enough that I allowed a single table lamp to burn and to cast a pool of soft, yellowy light across the bed.

I was completely calm as I waited for her, calm in the knowledge that it was time to even things out.

And then she came, hips swaying, into my room, tanned and looking utterly gorgeous. Her hair was again tied in a ponytail and it shone with innumerable sun-bleached shades.

'Oh, Mr Pearce!' she squealed delightfully, rushing over and wrapping her arms around my neck to hug me tightly. My ribs still ached as she squeezed, but in a way it really was good to see her and I couldn't deny that I had missed her too.

'Hello, Nurse Simmons,' I said for the very first time.

'Gosh, you're looking good,' she said, taking my hands in her own and stepping back to observe me better.

'And you too,' I said, because she really was. Better than ever, if that was possible. 'How was your holiday?'

'Oh, it was wonderful thanks,' she beamed with infectious enthusiasm. 'I had such an amazing time, and you know what's the best thing?'

'Tell me,' I replied, raising my eyebrows expectantly, even though she would have done so had I asked her to or not.

'Late last night, just as we landed back in

England, I dumped my stupid-arsed boyfriend,' she told me. 'I mean stupid-arsed *ex*-boyfriend,' she giggled, proudly jutting out those pert tits of hers.

'Good for you, Libby,' I said. 'It did sound as though you were ready to move on.' I actually felt a little sorry for the poor boy, and realised that he had probably been played just as relentlessly as me, and God knows how many other men.

'Yeah, he was an idiot all right.' She really did look incredibly sweet as she stood there grinning and swinging her hips from side to side, and for a split second I actually found myself doubting her cruel torment of three weeks earlier, but I was merely blinded by that innocent beauty and besides, my plan was soon to be set in motion. And then what Nurse Simmons said next was just too predictable, and so it began.

'Right, you need a bed bath!'

Clearly I needed no such thing; I was more than capable of looking after myself now, and had showered shortly beforehand.

'Okay, Libby, but please would you lock the door and draw the blind?' She gladly did as I asked before grabbing the wash bowl and heading on through to the bathroom, swinging her hips as she went.

I lay back against the pillows and smiled, actually looking forward to discovering what tease Nurse Simmons had in store for me this time, and she soon returned and set the bowl down in its usual place.

'Let's get you undressed, shall we?' she said brightly. I didn't have a pyjama top on, so she chatted away about her holiday as she untied the string of my pyjama bottoms and eased them down over my thighs.

Smirking to myself I watched her eye my lazy cock, lolling all soft against a thigh. I wondered if she was disappointed that I was not yet hard for her, and what she planned to do to resolve the issue. I didn't have to wait long to find out.

'So what do you think of my tan then, Mr Pearce?' I didn't bother to answer, as there was no real need. 'I don't suppose you can see much of it. Here, I'll show you a little more.' One by one Nurse Libby Simmons popped the press studs of her pristine white tunic from top to bottom, before allowing it to slip from her shoulders. She was braless and stood before me in nothing more than a tiny lace thong.

'I told you I needn't have bought the bikini top,' she said, nibbling her lower lip and playing it all cute and coy.

'So I see.' She did look incredible, I must confess, but I was not yet aroused and I actually caught her take an uncertain glance at my flaccid prick. But of course Nurse Simmons had other tricks up her sleeve.

'To be honest, for the last week I didn't even need the bikini bottoms either,' she went on.

'Oh?' I questioned, happily playing along with her little game.

She shook her head. 'No. One day me and whatsisname went off exploring around the island and we found a really secluded little cove. It was so beautiful and there was no one around, and so we just stripped off completely. Of course it made me incredibly horny as he rubbed me all over with sun cream, and I insisted on him making love to me in so many different ways beneath the sun. We ended up going back there almost every day. I did...' Libby bowed her head and actually managed to bring a blush to her cheeks as she stared at me with big doe-eyes, '...I did imagine it was you and not him I was *doing* it with, Mr Pearce.'

'Ah, that *is* nice of you, Libby,' I offered casually, and once again I caught her eyeing my cock, and although the idea of fucking Libby's stunning body on a beach was really starting to get me going, I was clearly not responding well enough for her liking.

'Look, I'll prove it!' she suddenly announced, playing her final hand and pulling down her panties to expose her shaved slit to me. 'No tan-lines at all!'

'Hey, you're right,' I replied. 'But turn around,' and she did exactly as I said. 'Hmm, I'm still not quite sure though. Bend over please.'

Why bending over would prove that she had been sunbathing naked was anyone's guess, but she complied unquestioningly all the same to offer me the view of her lovely cunt from behind. Once a flirty exhibitionist always a flirty exhibitionist, I guess.

'Okay, I believe you now,' I said, and she

stood upright once more and spun around to beam at me.

'See, I told you so.' Again she glanced at my groin, and this time she found satisfaction. 'Oh my, Mr Pearce!' she admonished theatrically, gazing at my fully erect cock with a calculating smile. 'But don't worry—'

This time, and with more than a hint of sarcasm, I finished the sentence for her. 'It's nothing you haven't seen before, right?'

Nurse Libby Simmons looked into my eyes and furrowed her brow. 'Hey, there's something different about you, Mr Pearce.' The penny seemingly still hadn't quite dropped.

'Well yes, there is, Nurse Simmons,' I announced, pulling up my pyjama bottoms and sitting upright to swing my legs over the side of the bed.

'You… you can talk!' she announced, that fact only just registering with her, and she stared with wide eyes as though witnessing some kind of a miracle. 'And… and you can walk!'

I stepped down onto the floor. 'That's right, Libby, and I can use my arms too. Look…' I reached out and slid her thong down her thighs until it fell to the floor in a tiny soft heap. 'Come,' I said, and she instinctively took my proffered hands.

'Where? What?'

'It's all fine, Libby. It's just that things are going to be a little different tonight. I'll be leaving hospital tomorrow morning, so for our final evening together, and as you've looked after me so well, I thought I'd repay your kindness.'

'But…' she blurted as I quickly lifted her by the waist and set her down on the edge of the bed.

'Don't you worry your pretty little head about it,' I soothed. 'I'm completely in control now,' and she allowed me to guide her onto her back with absolutely no resistance whatsoever.

I suppose she must have been too surprised to protest when I lifted back an arm and fastened the first leather restraint around the wrist. And by the time she could utter a quick 'Hey' the second strap was fixed in place too, both her arms now held securely.

My strength still had some way to go before I was fully recovered, but Nurse Simmons was such a neat little package that it was no problem for me to take her ankle against her steadily awakening resistance and fasten it to the foot of the bed. Then I grabbed her other leg, and she was really beginning to pull back now, but that too was quickly restrained and Libby lay naked and utterly at my mercy, four shapely limbs each secured to a corner of the ingenious hospital bed.

'Um, what…' she muttered uncertainly, testing her bonds a little and staring up at me with genuine concern in her eyes, 'what are you doing?'

I quickly moved to the head of the bed and stroked a loose strand of hair behind her ear. 'Hush now, silly,' I soothed. 'I just thought it might be a useful lesson – for your nursing, I mean – if you were to experience how it felt to be me. You have nothing to worry about; I'm simply going to treat *you* to a little bed bath tonight instead. Oh, but before I do there's just one last thing I need to do.'

Stepping back from the bed I walked over to where my towelling bathrobe lay draped across a chair, and slowly slid the belt through its loops until it came free. I had absolutely no intension of causing Libby any physical pain, and had already tested everything out on myself to discover its relative comfort.

Moving back to where she lay bound to the bed, I stretched out the belt with both hands and held it above her delicious, tanned, supine form.

'What the hell…?' she cried, but in doing so she only made things easier for me as quickly I slipped the improvised gag between her teeth, tying it tightly at the back of her head as she instinctively bit down on it. Of course she tried to resist, of course she struggled, but the whole manoeuvre took just a matter of seconds and then I was quick to soothe her once again.

'Relax, Libby, everything's fine,' I whispered. 'I promise I'm not going to hurt you. In fact, I'm only going to treat you to nice things, just like you did for me.'

Just like she did for me. Her big glossy eyes stared up and I could tell that she wanted to believe me, and for an instant I actually felt sorry for the poor girl and even considered untying her, but she really was a very naughty nurse and was in dire need of a good hard lesson.

Stepping back I dipped my hands into the bowl of clear warm water, before applying a generous squirt of soap onto a palm. 'I think you were right, Libby; those latex gloves are awful, so I'm going to use my bare hands on you too.'

Slowly massaging my palms together until thick suds began to squelch between my fingers, I finally pressed each one down against her tummy. Libby arched her back and released a muffled cry, her body stiffening at the contact, but as I slowly began to sweep them higher I felt her relax a little beneath me.

Staring down at her naked body I so wanted to ravage her completely, to run my hands across her exquisite curves, but that was not a part of my plan and I took my time, soaping ever upwards and teasing her with the gentlest caress.

Upon reaching her breasts I trailed my fingertips against their lower contours only, resisting the temptation to tease her more fully. Nurse Simmons shuddered and released a soft, muffled cry as I stroked her with the lightest of touches. I could see that her nipples had already swollen into two tight buds, yet I forced myself to ignore them and to continue sliding my hands higher still.

'You see, Libby, I knew you'd like it,' I said calmly as I gently soaped beneath her arms. 'This is just how you treated me, and it feels wonderful, doesn't it?'

Taking a clean flannel from the trolley I rinsed her upper body clean, once more ignoring all but the outer curves of her breasts, and Libby squirmed and whimpered her frustration.

'Right,' I exclaimed breezily, as though what I was doing to her was entirely normal, 'let's bathe your lower half now, shall we?' and immediately Libby's legs pulled futilely against her bonds.

I soaped each sun-bronzed leg, from her feet all the way up to her hips, allowing my fingers to splay and to trace along her inner thighs with each stroke. Over and over again my hands swept upward, moving that little bit higher every time, but never quite touching where I intuitively knew she wanted them to touch.

Just because I'd turned the tables, just because it was now my turn to tease her, it didn't mean I wasn't suffering too. I couldn't stop myself from staring at the swell of Libby's naked pussy and the neat line of her slit as it rose and fell with every involuntary lift of her hips. My cock stood hard and proud beneath my loose-fitting pyjama bottoms, and pulsated with an angry anticipation for what was to come.

In the end I took the flannel again and set about rinsing her off completely. At the last moment, once there was no trace of soap upon her naked body, and her newly tanned flesh glistened like honey, I lifted the damp cloth above her belly and slowly wrung it out until a fine trickle of warm water splashed down to snake its way between her thighs. Poor Libby moaned against the soft restriction of the gag and tensed the muscles of her backside hard, no doubt desperate to feel the water caress her body more intimately, but that was a satisfaction she was to be denied.

Carefully and tenderly I patted the gorgeous, captive nurse dry with a clean towel before smiling down at her. 'There you go, my dear,' I said, 'all done. It really does feel nice, doesn't it?' She stared up at me with a confused look in her eyes, but of course I ignored her silent plea completely.

'Oh my goodness!' I suddenly gasped, dramatically slapping a palm against my forehead. 'I've forgotten somewhere, haven't I?' Just as she had done with me I continued as though talking only to myself. 'But now the water's not warm enough and I would just hate you to catch a chill.' I furrowed my brow as though concentrating hard.

'I know,' I exclaimed. 'I remember what you did once to clean me up when we had no water, and well, I suppose I could do just the same for you.'

And before she had a chance to work out what the hell I was talking about I quickly leant down and sank my lips upon a rosy nipple, sucking deeply and bringing the swollen tip against my tongue. Once again Libby tensed her body and cried out as best she could, and despite the restriction of the gag it was plain to hear that her moans were born of pleasure and not from any form of discomfort.

I lifted my head away and circled my lips around her other neglected nipple, this time flicking my tongue and coating her dimpled flesh with my warm saliva.

Libby twisted against her bonds and I watched

with personal satisfaction as she tossed her head with a frustrated passion.

'Oh dear, I am silly, there's somewhere else I've forgotten,' I said casually, before taking a nipple between my teeth and slowly stroking my hand across the gentle hollow of her tummy, feeling her muscles tensed beneath my fingers. I curved my hand over the swell of her waxed mound, pressing the heel of my palm just above her clit, and immediately the heat of her body betrayed her desire.

Carefully I allowed my middle finger to work its way between Libby's wet, swollen lips, and her resolve gave in all too easily. I gently rubbed my fingertip along the length of her slit, up and then down again, smearing her silky juices as I went, and my naughty nurse tensed her buttocks hard, willing me to play with her still deeper.

My lips again circled around a nipple and I teased it very lightly with the tip of my tongue, and at the same moment I suddenly plunged my finger deep within her hot, wet cunt.

Libby uttered a muffled cry and arched her back as I slid my finger back and forth against her inner-wall, over and over again, but before I could allow her to enjoy her pleasure completely, I quickly and rather cruelly lifted myself upright, staring down at her with affected shock.

'Well, Nurse Simmons!' I admonished. 'You *are* a naughty girl, aren't you? Just look at how wet you've become.'

I pulled my finger from her pussy and held it up to the light so that it glistened, slick with her juices.

'But don't worry about it,' I continued, adopting a softer expression. 'It's nothing I haven't seen before.'

Of course it was a game, of course it was revenge, but I still wanted Libby's body as much as I ever did. It would have been so easy for me to fuck her right there, right then, and I have absolutely no doubt that she wanted exactly that too, but where would the lesson have been in that? I had waited weeks for this moment to arrive, and desperate though I was to feel her tight young pussy sucking around my cock, I simply had to take my time, to really savour the experience.

'Forgive me, Nurse Simmons,' I went on, 'but I've not finished my job yet, have I? There's somewhere else that needs licking clean.'

Lowering my face between her parted thighs I pressed my lips to the smooth swell of Libby's pussy, self-indulgently drawing in the musky scent of her arousal and feeling my aching cock throb in response. I alternated between planting delicate kisses against the slick flesh of her cunt lips, with teasing laps of my tongue, and she lifted her hips so that I might kiss and lick her more intimately still.

But I was in complete control now, and I continued to taunt her mercilessly, purposely teasing her clit with only an occasional feather-light flick of my tongue.

Libby began to release frustrated sobs and I couldn't help but feel sorry for the girl. So, and despite the fact that she deserved a far harsher punishment, I circled my lips around her clit and began to suck. I had to press down against Libby's thighs so she'd not inadvertently injure my still fragile jaw, such was the degree that she thrashed.

I alternated sucking, drawing her clitoris tight within the vacuum of my mouth, with lapping her with the flat of my tongue. Once again I used my fingers to enter her, two held firmly together, and Libby's pussy gripped me with a succulent wet heat.

I finger-fucked her slowly whilst licking her swollen bud, from side to side then up and down. Her delectable body was almost too easy for me to read, and as she tensed one moment, releasing a muffled squeal from the back of her throat, and relaxed the next, I worked her just the way I knew she wanted.

It was not long before I sensed the sexy nurse's climax fast approaching, and I taunted her harder and faster, lapping her clit and fucking her wet hole with straightened fingers. Her feet writhed against the sheets as she released muted cry after cry.

With one final, intense assault, and just at the very moment when I feared I might push her over the edge, I lifted myself away, panting and wiping my wet chin against the back of a hand.

Libby stared up at me with a look of absolute horror, and I was finally witness to what she must have seen in my eyes, yet teasingly chose to ignore, only a few weeks earlier.

'Christ, I'm so sorry, Nurse Simmons,' I said, 'I'm afraid I got a little carried away. Your delicious little pussy just tasted so sweet and I couldn't resist it. I'm not sure what came over me. Please forgive me.'

I smirked down at her, blatantly admiring the way her lovely breasts rose and fell as she tried to calm her agitated breathing.

'I must admit though,' I went on, 'it really is a remarkably tasty pussy, and I know this is an outrageous thing to ask of a nice young lady such as yourself, but do you remember when you allowed me to test how smooth it was with the tip of my cock? When you rubbed me up and down with it? You do? Well, would you mind if I was to try that again, now? It really did feel so nice.'

Libby moaned some kind of unintelligible affirmation and vigorously nodded her head, but even if she'd protested it would have made no difference as I fully intended to fuck her anyway.

'Thank you, my dear,' I crowed, 'that's very sweet of you.'

Quickly stepping out of my pyjama bottoms I stood their naked and unabashed, my cock rigid and curving outrageously up towards the flat of my stomach. I caught Libby staring wide-eyed, as I carefully climbed up onto the bed to kneel between her thighs, gripping my shaft in my fist and stroking it back and forth. Carefully I positioned myself over her, supporting my weight on a single arm, and then guided my cock against her exposed, vulnerable pussy.

She shut her eyes and whimpered as I pressed the bloated tip into her slit, and I too was forced to swallow hard as I felt her soft wet flesh envelop me. Pushing a little deeper I worked myself between her lips.

'Fuck me, Nurse Libby, you really do feel amazing,' I grunted, teasing her further still, 'but if only… if only I could enter you.'

As I knew they would her eyes immediately flashed wider and pleaded with me to do just that, but of course I ignored her in just the same way she had ignored me when in control of proceedings.

I began to work myself up and down between her sex lips again until the scarlet head of my cock ran slick with her cream. I aimed it at her entrance and she angled her hips to offer herself more blatantly. The lone arm that supported my weight burned like hell now, and it was not an act when I said, 'I'm sorry, young lady, but I can't hold myself like this any longer. My muscles are still too weak, but it would be such a shame to stop now.'

She quickly nodded her head in agreement and, smiling to myself, I moved on to the final stage of my revenge. 'But maybe, if I just rest like this for a little while,' and I pushed forward so that her body began to yield to me.

She really did feel incredible, and her wet heat begged me to press further. It was as much a torture for me as it must have been for her, but I certainly didn't intend to deny myself for much longer. Libby lifted her hips, encouraging me to enter her deeper, but with each of her thrusts towards me I would only pull away.

Then supporting my weight on both arms I stared deep into her eyes. 'You look beautiful, my dear,' I whispered, and slowly I began to tense and release the muscles of my arse so as to fuck her entrance only. 'You know, you were right when you told me before that it was such a shame we couldn't fuck. Can you imagine how good that would feel? But I really would hate to be responsible for you losing your job. Although, wouldn't it be lovely to see what it was like?'

Libby's eyes pleaded with me as she whimpered against the gag. 'Maybe we should try it, just once,' I goaded, and as she nodded her head impatiently I thrust my hips and buried my cock deep within her cunt with one smooth movement.

After weeks of pain and frustration I'm not sure that I have ever experienced a sensation more wonderful than Libby's tight cunt as it gripped me. Yet even now she gave in to her selfish side by quickly angling her hips and using her strong inner muscles against me. I could easily have succumbed to her, but I felt it was my duty to remain in control. And so almost as quickly as I entered her I pulled back until the tip of my cock was lodged at her entrance again, and I returned to taunting her with the subtlest of movements only.

Poor Nurse Libby's nostrils flared and her brow furrowed. She cried out as best she could, but I simply ignored her protests and continued with my unremitting tease. 'Fuck, that was amazing!' I gasped. 'It somehow feels so wrong for me to be doing this to you, but...'

Nurse Simmons groaned and threw back her head as again I thrust the full length of my cock deep inside her, adjusting the angle of my hips for deeper penetration, but just as before I quickly withdrew. The poor girl's eyes sparkled wide and flashed with frustration as I continued tormenting her, and really it gave me no pleasure to watch her suffer in such a way. It was time for the lesson to be brought to a close.

'I'm sorry, nurse, I just can't help myself, but just like with the latex gloves, if you don't tell then neither will I.'

I sank into her again.

Lifting myself up onto locked arms, aching and trembling though they were, I began to fuck gorgeous Nurse Simmons with long, deep strokes, sliding from the tip of my shaft all the way to the root, and out again.

Harder and faster I thrust, my abdomen slapping noisily against hers. Her lithe body felt just too damn good and the sensation of her hot wet cunt sucking tightly around my erection almost made up for her previous behaviour. Beyond the physical sensation of her body beneath me, the psychological element that I was finally taking what I had been owed for so long was enough to send thrill after spine-tingling thrill coursing through my body. Panting and grunting I willed myself to ignore the dull ache of my arms and to accept only the immense pleasures of her pussy, and with one last burst of energy I increased my pace.

I have no idea how close she was herself – I was entirely lost, and in that moment my plan could easily have gone wrong – but as I felt my orgasm surge I quickly withdrew from the moist heaven of her cunt, taking my prick in a fist and working it hard for a second or two, then I gave in, crying out as I began to spurt hot sticky cum all over the panting nurse's stomach and breasts.

The pleasure was simply far too great for me to be aware of anything beyond my own intense climax, but as I began to slow, to stroke my cock again and the last heavy drops splashed down on her tummy, I opened my eyes to view the mess I'd deposited on her exhausted body.

I had won. Revenge was finally mine. And as the last vestiges of pure animal pleasure slipped away from me I felt truly awful. I had lowered myself to her level, yet gained little satisfaction in doing so.

Climbing from the bed, avoiding her gaze as I did, I tried to justify what I had just done with the thought that it was no worse than anything she had subjected me to, and that Nurse Simmons really did deserve to be taught a lesson.

Quickly I dressed in the clean clothes I'd left hidden on the chair beneath my dressing gown, pulling on a pair of boots before turning to face the bed once more. She stared up at me, her eyes dull and her pupils as black as polished jet.

'I'm sorry, Libby,' I said, and really I was. But in a way I was grateful, too. Nurse Simmons had used me all right; she had made me the victim of her own peculiar little game, but even so I couldn't help but feel something for her. Had she known what she was doing by teasing me in such an outrageous manner? Of course she had. Had she meant to cause me any real distress? I'm not so sure.

I released one strap from around her wrist before leaning down to kiss her lightly on the lips. Then turning away, I left my room for good.

You see, earlier that afternoon I had officially been discharged with as clean a bill of health as I could have hoped for. I was so relieved that I had thought about leaving there and then, but knowing that I was so close to seeing Nurse Libby Simmons for one last time, knowing that really I was owed my revenge, I persuaded the ward sister to allow me to stay for one more night based on the lie that I had no way of getting home until the following morning.

And even now, two years on, I often find myself thinking about Libby Simmons. I often wonder if she's out there somewhere, playing her little games, and if she is, whether I should feel sorry for her victims or be envious of them. Mostly, though, I just look back on strange weeks in a peculiar phase of my life that was made that little bit more interesting by a unique and utterly remarkable young woman.

There was pain, there was fear and yes, there was frustration beyond belief, but would I have changed any of it had I been able to? If it meant missing out on meeting Libby Simmons, my naughty little nurse, then I'm not so sure that I would.

The Discipline Officer

Samantha was a spoilt brat, and proud of it. She could do whatever she pleased and there wasn't a soul in the world could stop her. Or so she believed…

She was a young woman now, and felt with all of her heart that every day spent in school was a day wasted when she could be out there having fun. Samantha would regularly question what the point in her education was anyway; it wasn't as if she would ever need to work. Her trust fund was set to mature as soon as she hit twenty-one, and she knew full well that the content of her father's wallet was never more than a well-timed hug and a fluttered eyelash away.

Over the years Samantha had used every devious trick in the book to get herself expelled from a succession of the finest girls' schools in the country. On the last occasion, her suggesting to the headmistress that she should perhaps, 'Get laid and then maybe she would lighten up a little,' to an audience of the entire sixth form, had proven to be the final straw in a long list of calculated and petulant misdemeanours.

Samantha had mewed to her father that it wasn't actually her fault that she kept getting thrown out of school, and went on to explain that none of them seemed to understand her quite the way that her *daddy* did. She had suggested that they perhaps forget about her schooling altogether, and that it might be a better idea to set her up with a nice little apartment in one of the more fashionable parts of town instead.

For once, however, things had not gone entirely her way as, although Samantha's father was something of a pushover where his daughter was concerned, he was nevertheless a principled man and was determined that his only child should receive the education his own humble beginnings had denied him. As a last ditch attempt to make that happen, he had called in a few favours and promised to make an enormous donation to the school gymnasium fund just so as to secure a place for his daughter at the very expensive *Saint Hilda's Boarding School for Young Ladies*.

Samantha had, of course, stomped and strutted, complaining bitterly that it just wasn't fair, before finally refusing point-blank to go. But by way of a compromise her father suggested that if she were to attend school and be expelled yet again, then he would finally allow her to put her schooldays behind her for good. If, on the other hand, she were to leave by her own volition, then he would cancel her trust fund and let her make her own way in the big wide world, just as he had done all those years ago as a penniless sixteen-year-old boy.

Consequently, Samantha grinned to herself in the knowledge that she would have Saint Hilda's packing her suitcases for her in no time at all!

Being summoned to the headmaster's office on her very first day at the new school was impressive, even by Samantha's standards. She'd seen him for the first time during morning assembly, and was actually pleasantly surprised by what she had found. He must have been in his late-forties and she thought him rather handsome in that 'older-man' kind of a way.

Samantha was well aware of the powers she wielded as an extremely attractive young lady, and she had decided that there might be some fun to be had in the process of getting herself kicked out. Of course, it would be a shame if his career was ruined in the process, but it wasn't as if Samantha could be entirely blamed if they just happened to be caught performing inappropriate acts in his study.

Saint Hilda's had a strict uniform policy, yet as she strolled casually along the corridor it was plain to see that Samantha was already flouting it outrageously. Her regimental school-tartan skirt was tiny compared to the other girls', and whenever she found herself needing to bend forward it proved to be downright indecent.

Her blouse was at least two sizes too small and she had buttoned it not nearly high enough at the neck. And as for the heels of her shoes, they must have been a good three inches higher than permitted under school law. Samantha's entire appearance could not, in all honesty, be considered decent for a young lady at Saint

Hilda's, but she knew that very well, and if it only ended up in hastening her expulsion, then that was just perfect.

Arriving at the headmaster's study some six minutes late for her meeting with him, Samantha knocked on the heavy oak door and entered. Inside was a reception area where a bespectacled secretary sat typing at her desk.

'Excuse me, I'm here to see the headmaster,' Samantha announced with exaggerated shyness, already practicing the Little-Miss-Innocence voice that had yet to fail her, while locking her hands behind her back and gently swinging her hips from side to side.

The secretary looked her up and down with a raised eyebrow, before smiling. 'Very well, let's see then, shall we? Your name please?'

'Samantha,' she replied. 'Samantha Nelson.' She watched as the secretary drew a painted fingernail across the open page of the headmaster's diary.

'No... no I don't think so,' she replied.

'Oh, but...'

'Wait a moment,' the secretary went on, 'I'm sure I can guess what the problem is.' She reached across her desk for a separate appointment book, before setting it down and flipping through the pages. 'Ah yes! Just as I thought; here we are.' She looked up once more, only this time without any hint of a smile. 'No, you are not scheduled to see the headmaster at all, young lady. You have an appointment with the discipline officer, and you're late!'

Something about the way the secretary's sunny demeanour suddenly evaporated caused Samantha's stomach to lurch unpleasantly. 'Who?' she quickly questioned, more than a little unnerved.

'It's "who" *miss*, and all in good time, young lady. Now, take a seat over there. You'll be called for soon enough.'

Samantha did just as she was told, as much out of confusion as compliance, and sat in silence with her brow furrowed wondering what on earth a 'discipline officer' could be, as none of her previous schools had ever had such a thing. Whatever it was, it did not sound promising.

She wasn't given long to consider the matter, however, as suddenly a buzzer on the secretary's desk startled Samantha out of her reverie.

'You may go through now, Miss Nelson,' the secretary announced, indicating a door to the right.

Samantha stood and straightened what little there was of her skirt to straighten. She took a deep, steadying breath and reminded herself that she was special, and could do absolutely anything she pleased, before stepping towards the door to turn the polished brass handle.

She found herself entering a large study that was very much in keeping with the grandeur of the school. Her heels clicked across polished wooden boards, and she looked up to see bookshelves towering all around her, each one brimming with leather-bound tomes.

An enormous marble fireplace dominated one

wall, and to one side sat an imposing, heavy oak desk, yet as Samantha peered through the gloom of the room, she could see no one sitting behind it.

She slowly peered around and was suddenly surprised to see a woman's form silhouetted against one of the large arched windows opposite. She was standing with her back to the room, clearly looking out over the playing fields which stretched away outside. And whoever she was, she did not turn to face Samantha when she eventually spoke.

'Come in, Samantha, and please be a dear and shut the door behind you.'

Samantha did just as instructed, rather confused by the peculiarity of the situation.

After a further period of silence, the tense atmosphere doing nothing to relieve Samantha's growing sense of uncertainty, the woman turned around.

She smiled warmly at Samantha and stepped forward with supreme confidence, while offering a hand in greeting. Samantha took it instinctively and stared, open-mouthed, without uttering a word. The lady was quite breathtaking. She was certainly beautiful, but there was more to it than that. She had a certain elegance about her that Samantha had never seen among the staff of a stuffy old boarding school before. But it was not just her natural good looks that were so striking; there was something strangely contradictory about the way she dressed. On the one hand she looked intensely formal, yet on the other she exuded a strange, elusive sexuality.

The discipline officer wore a tight cream-coloured blouse, which was buttoned all the way up to her neck and was set off with a string of beautiful, silver-grey pearls. She wore a long, very tight pencil skirt in dark grey, which was patterned with only the faintest of pinstripes. It was cut high in the waist and accentuated the curve of her impressive hourglass figure just perfectly. From what little of her legs were on show, Samantha could see that the she was wearing silk stockings, with an obvious seam that ran up the back of her calves, and she had no doubt that they would be fastened to appropriately luxurious underwear.

On her feet the lady wore patent leather stiletto heels, far more extreme than any Samantha had seen on a teacher before.

'Hello, Samantha, I'm very pleased to meet you,' the lady said. 'My name is Miss Grant, and I am Saint Hilda's discipline officer.'

There was something hypnotic about the icy-blue grip of Miss Grant's stare, and Samantha was not at all sure that she liked it. It almost felt as though she was being read, as though her most secret thoughts had been laid bare, yet unnerved as she was, Samantha felt quite powerless to look away. But eventually the discipline officer blinked softly and Samantha felt as though she could breathe once more.

'Please, do take a seat,' she offered, at last releasing Samantha's hand and indicating the straight-backed chair that stood to the front of the desk.

Samantha seated herself in silence. She watched, utterly transfixed, as Miss Grant stepped around the desk and lowered herself smoothly and effortlessly into her own chair. The discipline officer sat with perfect poise, the epitome of refined elegance previous schools had desperately, and unsuccessfully, tried to drum into Samantha. She picked up a pair of tortoiseshell reading spectacles and perching them on the tip of her nose.

'Lollipop?' she suddenly asked, lifting a huge glass jar from the corner of the desk and tipping it towards Samantha, who looked utterly affronted that anyone could possibly think a young lady of her age could be placated by something as childish as sweeties.

'Um, no thanks,' she mumbled in response.

'Suit yourself,' Miss Grant said, completely at ease. 'Now then, to business.' She reached for a rather thick dossier of papers and set them down in front of herself. Briefly she looked over the rim of her glasses and offered a smile, causing Samantha's stomach to lurch once more, before turning her attention to the folder.

Miss Grant really was a remarkable looking woman, and Samantha couldn't stop herself from studying her while she read. Her hair was a lustrous chocolate-brown, and although it must have been rather long, she wore it pinned up at the back in a way that would have looked incredibly severe on many women, yet somehow suited Miss Grant just perfectly and only added to her refined glamour.

Her eyebrows were meticulously sculpted and arched, her skin alabaster white, and but for a tiny chicken-pox scar on one cheek, entirely blemish free. Seemingly, the only concession that the discipline officer made to traditional femininity was in her decision to wear lipstick, yet even this was a shade darker than was perhaps obvious, and reminded Samantha uneasily of dried blood.

After a few minutes, which to the disquieted schoolgirl felt like an eternity, Miss Grant suddenly closed the file of papers with a dramatic slap, causing Samantha to jump with fright.

'Well now, Samantha,' she said, 'you *have* found yourself in a number of little scrapes over the years, haven't you?' Again her words were accompanied by that gentle smile. In a way it made Samantha want to trust her, yet at the same time it somehow made her seem that little bit more dangerous.

The discipline officer's words were of course a major understatement, as Samantha's records showed that she had been disciplined, suspended and ultimately expelled from more schools than you could care to shake a stick at.

'The good news, however, is that we do not care about previous misdemeanours here at Saint Hilda's,' the woman went on. 'All of our girls start afresh with an absolutely clean slate.' She paused and raised an accusatory eyebrow before continuing. 'But sadly, Samantha, on this your very first day here you have already chosen to blot your copybook. What was it now?' She reached across and picked up a memorandum from the desk. 'Ah yes. "Smoking a cigarette on school premises".'

Samantha thrived on confrontation. Her absolute belief that she could get away with anything calmed her and a tiny piece of Miss Grant's spell was suddenly broken. 'Yes, Miss,' she replied with a smirk.

The schoolgirl's arrogance only seemed to amuse Miss Grant, however, as she released a tiny snort of laughter. 'Well, full marks for honesty, I must say. I'm very impressed that you didn't try to blame it on one of the other girls.' There was a sudden, almost imperceptible shift in Miss Grant's expression that caused Samantha to stiffen on her chair. 'You are by no means unique, Samantha, and I have seen this kind of thing many times before. You were intentionally exerting what power you perceive yourself to have in a blatant and all too obvious manner; testing your boundaries, as it were. You knew full well that you would get caught and you knew full well that a confrontation would ensue.

'However,' Miss Grant continued, 'one thing I can promise you will not have been expecting, Samantha, was to find yourself brought before someone like me.'

Samantha had to concede to herself that this was more than the truth. Over the years she had become an expert at dealing with headmasters and headmistresses. The men were easy. Since she had blossomed into an extremely attractive young woman she had simply abused her sexuality to the point where they had no choice but to get rid of her for fear that they might actually submit to her manipulations and end up in serious trouble themselves. The women were a little harder, but so far they'd been so prim and so righteous that she had ultimately managed to shock them into dismissing her.

But Miss Grant was an altogether new challenge, and she gave the disquieting impression that she was totally unflappable.

'So what are you going to do?' Samantha goaded with mock bravado, as her heart raced unpleasantly. 'Expel me?'

Miss Grant laughed again. 'Good Lord no, Samantha. What on earth would give you that impression? I'm proud to say that in all the time I've served this school we have yet to dismiss a single girl, and trust me, I've had to deal with one or two characters who make you look like a little angel.

'But clearly I have to punish you; we cannot have our young ladies thinking the rules somehow do not apply to them, now can we?'

Under normal circumstances punishment meant nothing to Samantha. It only served to advance her that little bit closer towards her ultimate goal of expulsion. Detentions were an opportunity to humiliate the teacher in charge, and manual labour gave her the chance to miss classes and skip school all together. This time, however, there was something in the way Miss

Grant stared over the rim of her spectacles that let Samantha know things were going to be quite different.

'Um, what... what kind of punishment?' she asked, desperately trying to look un-phased, but failing quite miserably.

Once more Miss Grant's expression softened. 'Oh well, it's a little old-fashioned in a way, but I have found it to prove most effective.' Again the discipline officer paused to hold Samantha in her steely gaze, before going on without so much as a hint of embarrassment. 'I intend to give you a thoroughly good spanking, Samantha.'

'What?' Samantha blurted with absolute incredulity.

'Now, now, Samantha, it's "pardon, miss" if you did not hear me correctly. But on this occasion, as it's your first day, I'll forgive your indiscretion, although I do not expect to have to tell you again.'

'But... but you can't spank me!' Samantha exclaimed, incensed. 'It's... it's ridiculous. It's against the law and I'll... I'll tell daddy.'

The discipline officer was clearly amused by Samantha's sudden childish outburst, and she only just managed to disguise her amusement behind a crisp white handkerchief and elegant 'cough'. 'You really shouldn't be talking of "daddy" now, should you Samantha? If you consider yourself of an age to smoke cigarettes then you should surely be able to face your punishment like an adult too. Besides, your parents are entirely irrelevant here. It is me you answer to, and they cannot assert any influence over this establishment or me whatsoever.'

'What...?' Samantha began, but she was quickly and silently admonished with a raised eyebrow and a tilt of the head. 'I mean, pardon miss?'

'Good girl. That's a start. Now, if you had only taken the time to read the papers you were asked to sign upon joining us at Saint Hilda's, then you would have seen that we view you as being an adult now. If you do not wish to follow our regulations then you are free to leave at any time that you like. If, however, you choose to stay on, then you must obey all of our rules and that, I'm afraid, includes our choice of punishments.'

'You mean, I can just go?' Samantha asked with shocked wonder, suddenly delighted that she might not need to get herself expelled after all. 'I can leave here any time I like?'

'Right this very second if you so choose,' the woman confirmed. 'I'll even have a driver take you to the station.'

For one wonderful moment Samantha felt utterly elated, and she wondered what first to do with her newfound freedom, but then Miss Grant went on and spoiled things. 'Though I should probably point out to you, Samantha, that I am party to the – now how should I put this? – the, um, little *arrangement* you have with your father, and remind you that leaving Saint Hilda's on your own accord is in no way akin to you being expelled.'

Samantha's mind whirled with confusion.

'But... but if I go daddy will cut me off!'

The discipline officer gave a look of genuine empathy towards her charge, and even went as far as to reach a hand across the desk and briefly press it against Samantha's. 'I know, my dear,' she comforted, 'but as I say, you *are* a young woman now, and with adulthood comes responsibility.'

'But a... a *spanking*?' Samantha stammered, her indignation growing as she finally accepted she was beaten.

'Oh come now, Samantha, it's not that bad. It will be over and done with in no time. I can see by your school records that you're no stranger to physical pain.' She patted the file next to her with a palm. 'Admittedly it looks as though you tended to be the administrator as opposed to the receiver, but still...'

'But spanking?' Samantha repeated in a voice barely more than a whisper, and as much to herself as the beautiful woman sitting opposite her.

A moment passed in silence. 'So, my dear, have you made your choice?' Miss Grant prompted softly.

'Oh all right, just do it!' Samantha snapped, but then quickly remembering to whom she was speaking, she looked up shyly and added a quick 'miss'.

The woman nodded sagely. 'I think that's a very wise decision, Samantha, if I may say so.' She stood and stepped around her desk. 'Now, come,' she said, holding out her hands and indicating for Samantha to join her, and with a sigh of resignation Samantha reached up and allowed herself to be guided to her feet.

The naughty teenager was led across the room until she was left facing the large marble fireplace. Without the need for verbal instruction, the discipline officer carefully placed both Samantha's hands at shoulder width apart on the cold stone of the mantel. The fire in the grate must have died some time before, but the last vestiges of warmth comforted Samantha's naked thighs as she awaited her punishment.

'If you will just step a little further back, please Samantha,' Miss Grant directed, and Samantha obeyed until she was forced to support her bodyweight on her arms alone.

'I see you are wearing heels that contravene our uniform code,' the woman observed, 'and I really ought to discipline you for that too, but on this occasion I'm going to let it pass so as to make my task all the easier. And besides...' she continued in a conspiratorial whisper, '...don't tell anyone I said this, but I must admit they *are* rather nice shoes. Perhaps later on you could let me know where you found them. Now, legs apart please.'

Samantha suddenly felt very nervous. Never before had she been rendered so powerless, so utterly submissive to the will of another. The one nanny who had been foolish enough to raise a hand to her found herself dismissed just as soon as Samantha had run crying to her father. And there she now stood, an independent young woman awaiting the first proper spanking of her life, and she was scared.

'W-will it hurt, miss?' she asked meekly.

'Well I won't lie to you, Samantha,' the woman answered frankly. 'Yes, it will hurt. That's a large part of the reason why I choose this punishment, but it is certainly not the only reason. You will learn the rest soon enough.'

Samantha frowned as she tried to make sense of the discipline officer's words, but she had no time to draw any conclusions as she suddenly gasped at the sensation of her skirt being lifted and left bunched around her waist. Her chest heaved and she drew short, desperate breaths as she waited for the first spank to strike.

But what came next was not the stinging swat of an open palm, although it was no less shocking. Instead Samantha felt her white cotton panties being peeled down her thighs, to be left stretched between her knees. 'Hey!' she cried, through the shame of her exposure. With her legs strained wide apart, and with her wearing such an extreme pair of heels, she discovered a level of humiliation she had never known before.

'Oh come now, Samantha,' the austere woman scolded. 'How do you expect me to administer your punishment properly if your bottom is still covered?' And Samantha was given no time to respond as the first cruel slap suddenly came swinging down against a naked buttock.

'Ouch!' she squealed, and automatically tried to straighten up, but it only put an increasingly uncomfortable strain on her arms so she was forced to ease back into her previous position.

Again Miss Grant spanked Samantha's bare bottom, only this time on the opposite cheek, and if anything with an even greater force than before. 'Ow! Stop it, stop it please!' Samantha begged as she felt her flesh burn and throb.

Time and time again she was subjected to the crack of Miss Grant's hand smacking her naked bottom. Clearly the discipline officer was an expert at delivering a thorough spanking, as she moved smoothly and effortlessly from one cheek to the other to leave no area unpunished, swatting upward so that Samantha's cheeks would be lifted and parted ever so slightly with every cruel impact.

Samantha yelped and whimpered in tune with the torment of her spanking. While the physical pain was intense beyond words, soon enough, and somewhat strangely, it was no longer the worst aspect of her ordeal. That dubious honour fell to the simmering frustration that gnawed deep inside, and heightened with each slap from the discipline officer's hand.

She writhed as best she could, tensing and releasing her buttocks, but it was quite useless and the extra strain on her arms only added to her discomfort. She breathed rapidly and desperately, and her thoughts swam with strange emotions. Despite the fact that she was no longer a child she felt silent tears spill down her flushed cheeks, and in a desperate attempt to detach her thoughts from the physical assault, she discovered that it had little to do with the pain she was suffering, but more from an extreme dissatisfaction that throbbed deep within her body.

Each noisy spank of Miss Grant's palm stung just as the first, but in time, and somewhat bizarrely, Samantha found herself accepting the pain, longing for it even, as it offered a brief respite to the unfathomable anguish that swelled within her. She gritted her teeth and growled with the frustration that bit at her every nerve. She cried out and she moaned, yet deeper now and in a way that only added to her confusion. She tested her body further and was utterly perplexed to discover just how tightly her nipples had swollen within the confines of her bra. She looked further still and gasped with the discovery that she had parted her legs that little bit wider, dropped her upper body that little bit further forward, and in a way that meant the discipline officer was able to spank her more fully... and more intimately.

Samantha was a tough girl and she knew just how to deal with pain, but this was different. Her body felt as though it was on fire and she couldn't understand why she almost liked it. She had never before experienced the paradox of pain and desire mixing together. Normally the two emotions opposed one another, yet not here, not now. She found herself longing for her ordeal to be over, yet desperate to experience the next stinging slap that would cause an illicit thrill to charge deep into her core.

Panting heavily Samantha felt her body wind

tighter and tighter. She wasn't a stupid girl and she recognised the feelings; it was one she had enjoyed many times over the last few years, but never from an experience so humiliating and certainly not in the company of another woman. While Miss Grant's slaps continued to detonate on her poor punished buttocks, they were slower now, yet in contrast Samantha's tension only grew stronger.

She squealed tiny cries as the sensation of pain merging with pleasure became almost too wonderful to bear. She could feel just how hot and how tight her clitoris had swollen, yet she could not understand why. It was almost as if...

The naughty schoolgirl shut her eyes with absolute shame as the obvious reality finally presented itself. The beautiful discipline officer had been touching her while she spanked her. She knew it was wrong, but just as she had newly discovered that the divide between pain and pleasure was not always as clear cut as once it had seemed, maybe neither was that between right and wrong. But without considering it further she slumped forward to lean her forearms on the cool marble of the mantelpiece, offering her pussy more blatantly still to the bittersweet caress from behind.

The slaps still fell, but gently now. Miss Grant struck upward against the lower curve of Samantha's buttocks, and through it all the girl felt her clit being expertly teased by a fingertip.

'Are you comfortable, Samantha?' came the soft, comforting voice of the discipline officer, and the student simply nodded her head in response, unable to speak through her joy and disgrace.

In truth she was far from comfortable. Her backside burned and her arms ached, yet that was nothing compared to the confusion that raged in her head. But despite all of this she found it quite impossible to rebel against the exquisite torture she was being given.

'Well, I am glad. You see, Samantha, disciplining a young lady is not just about pain, you know.'

Samantha's mouth opened and she gasped as two fingers carefully work their way into her wet pussy.

'No, not at all,' the woman went on, her voice almost hypnotic. 'It's about showing her the kind of thing she might be permitted to enjoy if only she chooses to behave...' Samantha shuddered and released a long moan in unison with the sensation of Miss Grant gently fucking her with expert fingers, '...as much as it is about denying her when she's bad. I could very easily just stop your punishment right now...'

'Oh no, please,' Samantha quickly gasped, the idea alone a cruel torment.

'Or I could offer you more if you were to promise to be a better pupil in the future?'

Samantha noticed how Miss Grant had ceased spanking her, and now only soothed her aching flesh with deep, circular rubs of a thumb. 'Oh yes, please,' she pleaded.

'Of course, Samantha, if that is what you want.

But I need to know you're a good girl now. Are you a good girl?'

'Yes... yes I am, I promise,' came her pleading response.

'Yes *what*, Samantha?' the discipline officer prompted.

'Yes, miss... sorry, miss. I'm a good girl now, miss, I promise.'

'All right then, if you say so, and perhaps you do deserve a little treat now, but before I give it to you, you need to know one thing. This punishment is only ever given once to naughty girls. Thereafter it is occasionally awarded to those young ladies who display a certain level of maturity and who find themselves with a particular need. Is that understood?'

'Yes, miss,' Samantha gasped, furrowing her brow and pushing back her hips so that the discipline officer's fingers were forced to enter her still deeper.

'Very good,' the woman purred. 'And I must say, we do have a remarkable success rate here at Saint Hilda's, where persuading wayward girls to change their ways is concerned.' And with that Miss Grant proceeded to work her manicured fingers in and out of Samantha's wet pussy with an increased intensity, sliding her free hand around a thigh and using soft fingertips to caress her clit.

'Oh, God!' Samantha cried as shivering thrills shot through her over and over again. She drew rapid breaths through flaring nostrils, her legs suddenly weakening, and released a long, constricted squeal from the back of her throat. She panted and gasped. For some reason she found herself wanting to express the intensity of her passion through profanities, but at the same time she knew she'd promised to behave like a good girl now, and the possibility that the discipline officer might cease her special treatment, should Samantha start swearing, was one far too appalling to risk.

And then all rational thought was gone. Samantha's orgasm suddenly exploded with a blinding energy. It seized her body completely, caused her muscles to tense, a tingling energy sparking to her fingertips and toes. She slumped against the marble mantelpiece for support, fearing she might collapse at any moment; such was the exhausting intensity of her surrender.

It was as powerful a climax as Samantha had ever experienced, yet in time it moved into a second phase where she found herself releasing sobbing moans to the sensation of a softer, warmer state of bliss. Once more she focussed on Miss Grant's expert caresses, and the way she continued to stimulate her pussy, only very gently now.

Eventually it was over and Samantha released a shuddering exhalation as the discipline officer's fingers slipped away. She just stood there, far too ashamed to open her eyes, breathing deep, relaxing breaths while her heartbeat slowly began to settle. She felt the soft caress of her panties being carefully drawn up her thighs, of her skirt being pulled down and straightened with efficient hands.

As Miss Grant carefully helped Samantha away from the fireplace, soothing her tired arm muscles as she moved them to her sides, she spoke with her usual confident tone.

'Well done, Samantha,' she said. 'I have a good feeling about you. I don't expect to hear that you've been misbehaving ever again, and if I do I have many other punishments at my disposal, but none in quite the same vain as you've experienced here today.'

A finger stroked Samantha's flushed cheek, and she opened her eyes to meet Miss Grant's stare.

'I may be the discipline officer here at Saint Hilda's, but I'm not all bad,' she said. 'As you've discovered, I am quite capable of administering both pain *and* pleasure, and I'm happy to offer either depending on circumstances. From time to time you will be called to my office so we can review your progress, and appropriate punishments or rewards may be offered. And let me tell you, my good girls always leave those meetings with a smile on their faces. Is that understood?'

Samantha nodded shyly. 'Yes, miss,' she said politely.

Miss Grant smiled that beautiful smile and Samantha felt her heart skip one last time. 'Good girl,' she said, taking Samantha's hand in her own. 'Now, run along and I'll look forward to seeing you again very soon. And Samantha,' she added, peering over her glasses a little more sternly, 'no more cigarettes, please. Smoking is such an unattractive trait in a young lady.'

Samantha offered a brief nod by way of response, and the discipline officer gave Samantha's hand a gentle squeeze.

'Oh, and help yourself to a lollypop on your way out. I know very well that you want one really.'

'Thanks, miss,' Samantha replied, stepping to the desk on shaky legs and picking out a pink and yellow lolly from the jar.

As she popped it between her lips, tasting the sugary, strawberry goodness slip across her tongue, she walked towards the heavy oak door and reached for the handle. She turned to take one last look towards the discipline officer, but she was once more facing away, once more staring out of the large window at the playing fields beyond, and Samantha considered that it might not be such a bad thing to at least try and be a good girl. Well, for a little while, at least.

The Erotic Advancement of Little Red

Once upon a time, in a land far away, lived a beautiful young lady by the name of Little Red. Red wasn't her real name of course, and it had been many years since you could fairly describe her as being 'little', but it was what everyone had called her since the first soft fuzz of fiery red hair had appeared on her head as a babe in her mother's arms. There were only a few left in the village who could actually remember her real name, and even Red herself would have to think hard on it if ever she wished to be reminded.

As a child she had hated her red hair, as the boys in the village would pull at it and call her cruel names like 'carrot-top' and 'copper-knickers'. During her journey towards adulthood, however, its tone had progressively softened until it settled into a rich, lustrous auburn, which she would take great care over washing, scenting and brushing until it shone like a polished horse chestnut.

It wasn't only her hair colour that changed over those years either, as Red blossomed into an extremely attractive young woman. And those very same boys who had once teased her would now find themselves tongue-tied and awkward when in her presence.

Yes, Red was by far the prettiest young woman in the village. Beyond the long, silky-soft hair that now fell well below her shoulders, she had eyes as deep and as green as a millpond at sunset, a laugh that could melt the iciest of hearts, and lips full, soft and utterly enticing.

Red's body had developed too and was now as ripe and as juicy as a late summer pear. She was long in the leg and slim around the waist, she had curves just where they counted, and she'd been further blessed with a fine pair of breasts that were the envy of every woman over a certain age, and were often discussed in the smoke-filled corners of hostelries for many miles around.

Although Red's family owned a handsome, dapple-gray draught, a dairy cow named Thistle, three goats and a good dozen or so hens, times could be hard and her father kept a tight grip on the purse strings. This, much to Red's displeasure, meant that there was rarely money left over for little luxuries and what clothes she owned had been patched, darned and handed-down several times over. Consequently Red had become something of an expert with needle and thread, and although she always tried to look her very best, there was only so much even she could do to adjust a dress, a skirt or a blouse that she had simply grown out of two years prior. Thus her clothes would be that little bit tighter and that little bit shorter than was perhaps decent in a young lady of Red's shapely dimensions – a fact that was rarely complained about by the young men of the village.

Now, although Red was hardworking, intoxicatingly beautiful and generally kind of heart, she was not always the picture of innocence I may have led you to believe. She had never actually been with a man, of course, yet that certainly did not stop her from thinking about it. In fact, over the last few years Red would find herself imagining that very thought several times a day. And when that strange tingling sensation would take a hold of her senses, she was not at all averse to skulking away to the meadow – where the long lush grass would conceal her presence – so she could lie down on her back, lift up her skirt, and allow her hands to slip down between her thighs. Red would return to the farmhouse some time later, rosy-cheeked and with a look on her face that would have her mother worrying that Little Red had caught a chill.

She was an inquisitive girl, and over the years had become quite a student of the male physique. She'd obviously paid quiet attention to her older brothers as they grew from boys into men, and on several occasions had secretly observed the village lads as they washed naked in the stream. But by far her favourite lessons were learnt when she would creep out of the house late on a Friday night to peer through the windows of the old bunkhouse where the farmhands resided. Once there she would watch what the occupants got up to with the local girls they would bring home from the hostelries, drunk and full of amorous intent.

Red was a farm girl and therefore no stranger to the rutting of beasts, but at first it shocked her to witness sexual congress between a man and a woman. She had been surprised by the change in a man's *thing* – as she'd first known it called – as it grew from soft to hard, but soon she began to marvel at such magic and to wonder how it might feel if she were the one to offer it a tender caress. She would memorise the vulgar words she'd heard gasped in the throes of passion, and would take secret pleasure in repeating them aloud to herself when no one was there to hear.

Red had watched in awe as the village sluts took stiff cocks into their mouths, and how they would suck on them until the men would cry out and spill their sticky white cum across their chests. She had watched them fuck in all kinds of positions and had even seen a man use his tongue to lap a young lady's pussy – a young lady who, incidentally, looked an awful lot like the vicar's daughter.

That had been her absolute favourite new word; 'pussy'. She thought it so fitting, as she'd discovered her own to be just as soft and just as tender as a newborn kitten. On those nights when she would observe the farm workers at play she would inevitably find her own palm sliding beneath her nightshirt, where it would tease her clit in just the way she liked while she imagined it was *she* in there with them and that it was *her* body they were making use of. Soon enough Red would be forced to bite hard against a knuckle so as to stifle the cries of pleasure she'd unfailingly release before she would dash back across the darkened yard and quickly on up to bed.

Poor Red longed to experience a man for herself. While her friends would giggle and pull faces at how disgusting it all sounded, Red's eyes would mist over and she'd dreamily imagine how sweet it would be to close her lips around a gentleman's big hard cock and to suck on it until he was forced to groan with the pleasure she had bestowed.

There was one experience that Red dreamed about more than any other, however; more even than having her pussy licked by a handsome farm boy. Red desperately wanted to feel a man inside her. She wanted to experience the sensation of her pussy being stretched by a rigid shaft as it pushed slowly inside. She wanted to feel it consume her body entirely so that she'd be forced to cry out like all those women she had secretly observed. Poor Red desperately wanted to experience the joy in being fucked good and hard, but alas she was not married and nor was her father looking to find her a suitor for a good while yet – it was simply too useful for him to have an extra pair of hands around the farm – and so, for now, she just had to make do with the pleasure of her fingers and the occasional candle she would steal away when mother was not looking.

Now, I must warn you not to feel too sorry for Little Red, as in all honesty she couldn't always be described as being a 'good girl'. You see, over time she had become something of a tease. It began quite by accident one Saturday evening when she was called down to the kitchen by her mother for her turn in the tub. Red loved bath night and once mother had disappeared up to her room she would light as many candles as she could lay her hands on, hang a freshly laundered nightshirt in front of the stove and pull off her clothes before sliding naked beneath the warm water.

On this particular evening Red had been laying there, lazily dreaming of the ironmonger and how impressive his arm muscles looked as she'd watched him hammer out a new set of shoes for Snowflake, when she was startled out of her reverie by a sudden noise from outside. Her immediate reaction had been to fold her arms tight across her breasts so as to protect her modesty, but as she heard what sounded like an irritated whisper from beyond and beneath the kitchen window, she became aware of an all-too-familiar throbbing sensation between her thighs. Red shut her eyes and allowed her arms to slip back to her sides once more. She listened intently over her racing heartbeat, and again she heard the unmistakable sound of hushed male voices. Swallowing awkwardly through a constricted throat, Red called out – but only loud enough so that her peeping-Toms would be able to hear – 'Yes, mother, but I just need to stand up and soap myself down,' and on shaky legs she lifted herself upright.

At first she faced away from the kitchen window, but she could see just enough of its reflection in the polished copper bottoms of the pots that hung from the stove. And soon enough the shape of two heads presented themselves, quickly joined by a third.

Red was absolutely horrified that she was being spied upon – quite neglecting to acknowledge her own hypocrisy – yet as she proceeded to lather her breasts, discovering just how tight her nipples had now swollen, and the way they tingled as her fingertips played across them, she could not deny that there was something intensely thrilling about the experience.

Slowly she began to turn around. Not wishing to scare her voyeurs away she made sure to avoid facing directly towards them, yet positioned herself in such a way that they would be able to see all that any red-blooded male could possibly desire. Red took great care over soaping her naked body, twisting first one way and then the other, her creamy-white flesh dripping wet and shiny in the warm glow of the candlelight, her nipples flushing an angry shade of scarlet from the heat of the water. She allowed a palm to slip down between her thighs, and she rubbed back and forth against the soft fur of her mound. Red gasped as a fingertip ran across the tiny bud of her clitoris, to discover just how it had swollen and how much it longed for caresses. She even considered sliding a finger inside, to seek illicit joy in the heat of her wetness, but just as she was wondering if she really dared there was an almighty crash from beyond the window. Instinctively she looked up with fright, just in time to catch the startled expressions of her brother, Josh, and two of his friends a moment before they ducked away to disappear into the night.

Back in her bedroom Red was utterly incensed that her own flesh and blood could permit others to watch her as she bathed, but at the same time a tiny flame had been ignited, and once she'd climbed beneath the sheets she couldn't help but allow her fingers to slide between her legs to play with her pussy until she arched her back and struggled to suppress the cries of her passion.

Early the following morning Red sneaked into Josh's room while he was out tending the goats, with the intention of placing a rotten egg beneath his bedclothes by way of revenge. Upon lifting his pillow away, however, she discovered a soft leather pouch containing a good ten pennies; way more money than Josh could ever have earned through honest labour alone, and she quickly realised that the enterprising little worm had been profiting through his sister's bath time performances and she was quite set to explode with rage.

She immediately stuffed the pouch into her pocket and strode purposefully from his room, but just then, upon reaching the top of the stairs, for some strange reason she stopped short. It certainly didn't bother her that Josh would be in trouble beyond his wildest dreams should she complain to her parents, but it was more that she knew just what a puritan her father could be, and that once informed he would no doubt only then ban her from bathing in the kitchen where there were windows to be peered through.

She considered confronting Josh directly and demanding the money for herself, but then there would be no more shows for her to put on, and if truth be known she had rather enjoyed it. So with her mind made up she counted out exactly half of the pennies and placed them in her pocket. She then returned to Josh's room and replaced the pouch where she'd found it. Of course her brother would be incandescent with fury when he discovered half of his ill-gotten-gains were missing, but he would be in no position to protest, and being the young entrepreneur that he clearly was, he would no doubt only be encouraged to set about earning yet more.

Neither Red nor Josh ever discussed their little business arrangement, but thereafter, every Sunday morning, Red would go to his room and help herself to half of the contents of his pouch; a sum which only grew with time and the notoriety of her displays.

You might have thought that her bath night performances would have been enough to settle her appetite for male attention, but in time this proved not to be the case and she took to teasing the farm boys without any hope of financial reward. On summer afternoons she would choose one lucky young man, and let slip how sticky-hot she was and how she couldn't wait to sneak off when father wasn't watching to enjoy a refreshing dip in the creek. Once there Red would strip naked and dive into the cool water knowing her young voyeur would be hiding behind a tree while she frolicked in the water or sunned herself on the rocks.

Once a year the travelling folk would come to the village for the horse fair, and in the hope of earning a little extra money they would move from farm to farm in search of casual labour. These men had a reputation for being fighters, drinkers and frequenters of whores, and most farmers would threaten to set the dogs on them if they so much as dared to step onto their land. But not so Red's father as he knew them to be strong men and hard grafters, and on good years he would take on a dozen or so to help out in the fields.

During the traveller's most recent visit, Little Red had awarded herself the task of taking out their lunchtime refreshment, telling her mother that it was only fair that they be treated like any other farm worker, but secretly, she only did so because she enjoyed the attention they would bestow upon her, not to mention the pleasure she would gain from seeing them stripped down to the waist and glistening with the sweat of their toil.

Most of the local girls were scared of the travellers as they looked quite different to the men of the village. Their hair was as black as pitch and they would grow it long and wear it tied back with fine ribbons. Their skin was the colour of cinnamon bark and many had strange symbols and patterns cut into their flesh. The old wives would say this proved them to be in league with the devil, but Red refused to listen to such scurrilous nonsense, and anyway, even if it was true it only excited her further to chance her luck with such dangerous men.

On one particularly hot day, Little Red went to the men damp with sweat and clutching a cloth-wrapped cheese and a newly baked loaf to her chest. The leader of the group, a particularly handsome man with sapphire-blue eyes, rippling chest muscles and brass rings in his ears, thanked her in an accent so thick Red thought he might have come from the moon, and went on to say that, as she looked in need of a drink, they would be honoured if she stayed for a while and shared a draft of their ale.

Red had immediately thought to say, 'Thank you, no,' in the knowledge that her father disapproved highly of ladies who drank alcohol, but the beer looked ever so inviting, and as she watched one of the men pour it from a small oak barrel into enormous clay jugs, she found herself wetting her lips and offering an accidental, 'Yes please, that would be very nice,' instead.

In words she could make no sense of the leader quickly instructed one of his comrades to bring over a mug, and being the thirsty girl that she was, she immediately knocked back an enormous draught, only to then cough and spit it out through the shock of such a bitter taste. This caused the travellers to hoot with laughter and Red, thoroughly shamed, had half a mind to run away. But with a kind smile the leader held up his hand and told the men not to be so rude to their guest, before explaining that she must not gulp down ale in the same way she might enjoy her milk. He then went on to teach her to take small sips and to hold the liquid against the back of her mouth rather than at the front, and soon enough Little Red was drinking down the beer as though she had done so for years.

Before she reached the bottom her mug was refilled, and while they ate and drank together the men regaled Red with tales of their homeland. Red's mug was filled a third time, and as one particularly jolly fellow danced a side-splittingly funny jig, she noticed just how wonderfully fuzzy and fluffy the world now appeared. She told the men all about their reputation within the village, and they just laughed and agreed that it was probably quite fair. But she didn't think so at all; she thought them to be fine gentlemen for sharing their refreshments with her, and she gladly accepted another fill of the ale.

In time the leader asked her why on earth she was wearing so many clothes on such a hot day, and with a foolish grin Red threw out an arm to strike him across the chest. She told him not to be so stupid, as in a blouse and skirt she could not possibly be wearing any less. The man furrowed his brow and questioned why not, as where he and his friends came from it was just as normal for a lady to remove her shirt beneath the heat of the sun as it was for a man. Through hooded eyes Little Red giggled at the idea, and taking another sip from her mug, she proceeded to furnish herself with an enormous frothy moustache, much to the amusement of her newfound friends.

'That's just shilly,' she slurred. 'You're telling fibs.' But the men quickly assured her that it was absolutely the truth.

After yet another top-up, and the men pressing the idea on her further, Red hazily began to think that it actually wasn't such a strange idea for a young lady such as she to remove her blouse, as it really was a very hot day. Apart from anything, if it was what the womenfolk did where the travellers came from then where could possibly be the harm?

With a final few charmed words of encouragement from the men, she agreed that it would be nice to feel the breeze against her shoulders, and so she set about unbuttoning her blouse, an act that had once seemed so simple yet for some reason was now fraught with difficulty. Soon enough, however, and with the kind help of the leader, Red's shirt was removed and she sat as naked from the waist up as any there. It felt a little strange to begin with, to expose her breasts to a group of men, but she reminded herself that it was quite normal where they came from, and besides, they were all extremely complimentary, declaring that Red's could well be the finest pair they had ever set eyes on, and how pretty her nipples looked standing all rosy and pink.

As the last of the ale was shared out the leader, in a hushed tone, asked Red if she believed in magic, to which she hiccupped and replied, 'Of coursh I don't. Stories about magic are jusht for children.' The men muttered amongst themselves disapprovingly, and one or two even went as far as to make strange gestures with their fingers against their foreheads. The handsome leader looked deep into Red's eyes and told her that she should not talk about magic in such a way, as it was bad luck to do so. He explained that magic was all around them, in the wind, in the trees and even in the soil where they sat, and as if to prove his point, he quickly leaned forward, reaching a hand behind her ear and produced a shiny new penny, which he pressed into her palm.

Red was absolutely astounded and demanded he do it again, but he explained that such a gift was a sacred power and could only be used sparingly. He did offer to show her another enchantment, however, and making her stand with him he stepped back and muttered an incantation to the skies before quickly clapping his hands together twice, whereupon Red's skirt dropped to the ground to leave her standing in her drawers only. The workers laughed and whistled, and in a way that Red thought rather cruel, but before she had time to decide whether she was affronted or not the leader apologised for his silly trick, offering her a white-toothed smile that had way more powerful an effect on her than any of his silly 'magic'.

With a sudden frown he looked first to Little Red's left shoulder and then to her right, declaring with genuine concern that her beautiful skin was burning beneath the heat of the sun, and looking down she could see that he wasn't wrong. She suggested that she pull her blouse back on, but with a quick instruction to one of his men the leader told her that before she did so he had a soothing balm he should first apply.

Red had heard talk of the travellers' skills with herbs, and she was intrigued to see what was inside the tiny cork-stoppered flagon the leader was quickly handed. He explained to her that it was a secret concoction known only to travellers, and was made from a blend of fine oils and a combination of rare and precious plant extracts that could soothe even the deepest of wounds. Holding the flagon up to her nose he encouraged her to inhale its scent, and taking a cautious sniff, Red discovered it gave off a strong yet not at all unpleasant aroma. The leader explained that although it might feel a little strange, a man touching her naked flesh, only a traveller versed in the ways of ancient medicine was allowed to apply such an ointment, and he stepped behind her without giving her chance to question him further.

Red gasped and tensed her muscles as she felt his fingers press against her shoulders, but she was quickly soothed by his soft words and the cool, fragrant balm, and he proceeded to carefully smooth it first one way and then the other. She couldn't help but notice the contrast between his strong, calloused hands, as they moved lower to press into the tight muscles of her upper back, and the silk-like caress of the oil, and she closed her eyes and released a sigh of pure rapture.

Soon his fingers moved lower to rub the base of her spine, and then around her waist so that his palms ran across her belly. 'Oh!' Red gasped. 'I... I think I'll be fine now, thank you,' but the leader only continued, allowing his hands to travel higher. She could feel his groin pressing into her bottom, his strong arms enveloping her from behind, and she felt powerless to resist, even though she knew well that she should. She gasped and arched her back, pressing against his strong chest as his fingers began to stroke around the lower curve of her breasts.

'No really, please...' she panted, as his cupped palms moved up to smooth the salve directly over her nipples. His mouth was against her ear and it caused a shiver to run the length of her spine as he whispered in that thick, seductive accent that she should just relax and allow the ointment to work its magic. And swallowing hard Red did just that, whereupon he began to repeatedly pull her nipples with fingers and thumbs and in a way that would probably have hurt had it not been for the slippery nature of the oil, and as a result, it only felt good.

Red could picture how her nipples would look – she'd seen them that way many times from her own teasing – but she dared not open her eyes to witness it for herself.

The handsome traveller began to run his hands all over her breasts, lifting and squeezing until they were thoroughly coated in the balm. Red felt certain that it must be wrong to allow a stranger to touch her in such a way, but she kept on reassuring herself that he was a medicine man and was simply tending to her slightly burnt flesh. But as she felt his hands slide lower once more, down over her flat stomach, as she felt a gentle tug at the bow holding up her drawers, she could no longer kid herself that all was quite so innocent.

'No!' she gasped through a dry throat as she felt her underwear slip down her thighs. Her eyes flashed open and she saw how the men had closed in around her, and that they were grinning and wetting their lips as though presented with a wonderful feast. She felt one of the leader's strong arms close tight around her waist while the other slipped down between her thighs. She made an attempt to pull away, but he held her so tightly and again he whispered that all was well and that she should simply enjoy the effects of the soothing oil. And she wanted to believe him, but the look on the other men's faces told her a different story, and as a finger pressed firmly and she felt her pussy lips begin to separate she drew a breath to protest, when all of a sudden a shout came from the back of the group.

Red was immediately released, and she looked down to see first her drawers and then her skirt being quickly pulled back up her legs. Her blouse was draped around her shoulders and her arms thrust through its sleeves without so much as a trace of the careful caresses she'd experienced just a moment before. With a final hiss against her ear she was told that her father was on his way, and that if he was to catch her with the men he would have her guts for garters. And with a quick slap of the arse she was told to run, and to come back and see them again very soon.

So on unsteady legs Red dashed away to the woods at the edge of her father's land, clumsily trying to fasten the buttons of her blouse as she went.

When later she returned to the farmhouse, having slept off the effects of the ale in a hollow at the foot of an old oak tree, it was to a monumental scolding from her father. Under threat of a lashing he demanded to know where she'd been and what she'd been up to, whereupon she explained that having served the workers their refreshment she felt so flushed with the heat that she headed off to the creek for a dip. Both shocked and impressed by how easily she could lie, she went on to say how she must have fallen asleep through the heat of the afternoon sun and promised to make up for the chores she'd missed ten times over. Her father grudgingly accepted her apology, but with a suspicious glance he told her she was no longer permitted to take lunch out to the travellers.

Later that night, as the moonlight streamed in through her open bedroom window, Red lay awake realising how stupid she'd been to be tricked so easily, and what a lucky escape she'd had. But at the same time she could not stop her fingers from sliding down to you-know-where, to rub her clit while she imagined the men in the field and what they might have done to her naked body had things turned out only a little differently.

And so, dear reader, you will now expect me to tell you that Little Red's experience with the travellers taught her a valuable lesson, but alas that is something I am unable to convey. If anything, that experience only added to her frustration and encouraged her to behave just as badly as ever. Only a few days later saw her explaining to the neighbouring farm lads how she fully intended to take a trip to the creek for a bathe later that afternoon as the mountain water worked wonders on her hair. Inevitably, and not terribly subtly, the young men followed on behind, but upon reaching the creek she discovered that it was already taken by the baker's wife and her two fat brats. Red kicked at the dry earth angrily as she would now have to forgo her little tease, until it occurred to her that the Foss was only another half a mile or so upstream, and so with no little annoyance she continued on her way, turning every so often to check that her young trackers were still in tow, yet giving them just enough time to dive behind the nearest gorse bush or rock.

The Foss was a small waterfall at the very edge of the old forest. The water was much cooler here as it was deeper, and had little chance to have been warmed by the sun, but for a strong swimmer such as Red it was a wonderful spot for a dip. And no sooner had she arrived at its banks than she peeled off her clothes and dived in.

Red slipped through the water like a little otter, gasping from the cold each time she came up for air. After a short while she climbed carefully across the slippery rocks at the base of the fall, while taking a casual look to see if her audience was still with her. At first she began to wonder if they'd given up and gone home, but soon enough she spotted them tucked away behind a fallen tree. She stood in the spray of the cascade, naked and utterly brazen. She rinsed the thick main of her hair in the fall, before pulling it back and allowing it to slap in a thick rope between her shoulders.

She eventually dived back into the pool, only to resurface on the far bank. Climbing from the water she felt utterly invigorated and even offered a silent thank you to the baker's wife for her enforced change of plan. She wandered back up to where the lush meadow met with the big flat stones, before settling herself down in the soft grass.

After such a refreshing swim Red no longer really cared about the farm boys, but that did not stop her thoughts from inevitably turning to that one thing she wanted to experience more than anything else in the world, and she soon lay down on her back. The late afternoon sun warmed her naked flesh and she parted her thighs to accept its caress more intimately still. A gentle breeze teased the beaded moisture upon her milky flesh, and caused goose bumps to rise on her arms. She allowed one hand to trace across the soft contours of her body, and she liked what she found.

Now, although I may not have painted young Red in the best of possible lights, I should say that up until this point she had only ever displayed her body by way of a tease, and that she'd done so behind a certain, if poorly drawn, veil of innocence. On this occasion, however, Red's display moved onto a whole new level, and well aware that she was being observed she began to touch herself, cautiously at first, but then with greater and greater abandon. She desperately needed to experience a man, and as she lay there in the grass, frigging her poor neglected pussy for all it was worth, she only wished that those two stupid boys would come down and just take her.

She would have made it so easy for them. Obviously she would protest and she would struggle, but she would not have fought hard and if questions were asked she would have said it was hard to tell with the sun being so low in the sky. But she'd chosen farm boys for her prey, and boys they clearly were, as despite the fact that she was lying naked and fucking herself with two fingers neither dared to join her, to give her what she truly desired.

Little did she know, but on that fateful afternoon, when she finally brought herself to a shuddering climax, her little performance was not only being enjoyed by the two farm boys crouched with cocks in fists behind the fallen tree. No, not at all. There was another watching that day, and he was every bit the real man she dreamed of. He was big, he was strong and he was dangerous, but Red knew not that he was there.

A moment later, as she tried to steady her breathing, her fingers still held tight between her pussy lips, a great howl shattered the lazy afternoon silence of the forest, and suddenly startled she hurriedly dressed and dashed off home without so much as a glance to see if the farm boys were behind her.

Later that afternoon, while Red helped her mother prepare a stew for supper, she casually asked the question that had been troubling her since she scurried back down the hill from the Foss. 'Mother,' she began, 'are there wolves in the old forest?'

Her mother laughed. 'Of course not, you silly thing. The wolves were all driven back into the mountains many years ago.'

'But I could have sworn I heard one this afternoon,' Red said, pausing halfway through chopping a carrot and furrowing her brow.

Her mother continued to stir the broth on the stove before going on with a smile. 'Well perhaps you didn't hear *a* wolf dear, but you heard *the* Wolf.'

This only added to Little Red's confusion, and she looked at her mother with a frown. 'But I thought you said…'

'The Wolf is not actually a real wolf, although one or two old crones with too much time on their hands will gladly tell you that during the full-moon he will take on the shape of a giant beast and come stalking into the village looking for a young virgin to take back to his lair.'

Red looked at her mother through wide eyes, both terrified and excited by the tale. 'But, but is he real, have you seen him?' she quickly asked, and her mother looked wistfully into her steaming pot before going on.

'Oh, he's real all right, but he's no more magical than you or I. I saw him once when you were just a little girl. I was taking a pie and an arrangement of flowers over to the church in readiness for Harvest Festival, and your father had asked me to stop by Jameson's to pick up a new axe handle he'd ordered. I was in the store asking the old man how his daughter was getting on with her new babe, when suddenly the door burst open and it seemed as though all daylight had been sucked from the room.'

Little Red felt the hair on the back of her neck stand on end.

'The look of terror on Jameson's face was an absolute picture, and it was enough to have me quickly spinning round to see who, or what, had just entered. And there he stood, towering over me with a good six or seven deer skins slung beneath an arm as though they were no heavier than a basket of strawberries.'

'But what was he like?' Red excitedly implored. 'Was he handsome?'

Red's mother smiled to herself before continuing. 'Yes, you could definitely call him handsome, but perhaps not in the traditional way. He looked big and strong like a real man should. You could see why they called him the Wolf, as his hair was rather shaggy and more grey than black. He can't have shaved in over a week as his beard was thick, but for three long lines running diagonally across one cheek where no bristle would grow. I've heard it said that they were scars gifted to him by the last lone wolf to roam the forest, when they came across each other one moonlit night and were forced to fight for dominion. He wears an enormous fur cloak on his back too, and some claim it is the hide of that very same beast.' She stared dreamily into the steam rising from the pot. 'His eyes were more animal than human, too, as they were a very pale blue, and the way he looked at me gave me the unnerving impression he was sizing me up, seeking out my weaknesses, and it caused my poor heart to skip a beat.'

'What did he say?' Red pressed eagerly.

'Nothing; I didn't give him chance to. To my shame I simply ran from the shop, forgetting father's axe handle completely.

'But there's a lot of nonsense spoken about the Wolf if you ask me,' she continued. 'I'd say he's just a man who prefers his own company, and who can blame him for that? But either way he's different to folk round here, and that makes him dangerous. Some say he keeps a cottage deep in the forest, but I've never known anyone who's ever seen it.

'Anyway, young lady,' Red's mother went on, turning and facing her daughter with hands on hips, 'what were *you* doing near the old forest that you might, or might not, have heard a wolf howl?'

Red quickly turned and applied herself once more to her chopping. 'Oh, nothing,' she said with all the bluff innocence she could muster. 'I… I just went up to the Foss for a quick dip.'

'Well you mind what your father's told you about going near that forest,' mother scolded. 'There's bad men and wild beasts in there would like nothing more than to chomp on a pretty little thing like you.'

'Yes, mother,' Red dutifully replied, and her mother stroked a palm across her cheek.

'You're a good girl really, Little Red,' she sighed, offering her a smile of pure affection. 'But I do smell trouble with you. Now, come on; we'd best get on and finish this stew before the men get back all hungry and in need of feeding.'

That night Red dreamt of a great wolf stalking through the farmyard, its wet nose sniffing at the ground as it searched for fresh meat. She instinctively knew it was her it was hunting, and as it raised its shaggy mane and offered a howl to the moon she suddenly awoke, heart racing and drenched in sweat, to hear what she could swear was the last of a beastly cry echoing down across the valley floor.

That following Sunday, like every Sunday, Little Red and her family pulled on their finest clothes and headed up to the church. In Red's case this meant she was wearing a beautiful white linen dress embroidered, by her own fair hand, with pretty spring flowers. She loved that dress dearly, but it really was far too small for her now, and as she respectfully sang the chosen hymns she found herself in grave danger of bursting out of it every time she took a breath, thus very nearly offering the congregation a practical lesson in the sins of the flesh.

The vicar's sermon was as mind-numbingly boring as usual, and in order to entertain herself Red took to crossing and uncrossing her legs in front of the altar boys, giggling to herself as she watched them fail in their duties because of their staring.

Once the service was over Red couldn't wait to get back to the farm to tuck into lunch, but her mother quickly poured cold water on that particular plan by telling her that she had just received word that grandmother had been taken ill and that Red was now charged with the task of taking a basket of provisions to her cottage. Little Red moaned and complained bitterly, but her mother scolded her for being such a selfish girl, yet went on to assure her that there would be an extra large portion of pudding set aside for her return.

Back at the farm Red was about to go change into something more comfortable for the journey when mother told her just how pretty she looked in her Sunday best, and that it would warm granny's heart no end to see her favourite grandchild so well turned out. Handing her a basket of goodies she instructed her to pick a bunch of wild flowers along the road, and with a quick peck on the cheek she sent her on her way.

But just as Red scuffed her feet up the dusty path her mother called out to her once more. 'Oh, and don't you be taking any shortcuts through the forest, young lady, you hear? You keep by the road!'

Now, on this particular Sunday there was not a cloud to be seen in the sky, the sun beat down without remorse, and it wasn't long before Red felt the first beads of sweat gather in the shadow between her breasts. To make matters worse, she had foolishly pulled on a particularly itchy pair of drawers that morning, and through the heat of the day they began to chafe her delicate thighs. Soon she couldn't take it any more, and with an exasperated squeal and a stomp of her foot she stopped still and dropped the basket to the ground. She looked first up the road and then back down the way she had come, and seeing there was not a soul in sight, she quickly slipped off her underwear and stuffed them into the basket. The sense of relief as she continued on her way was monumental, and she found herself rather enjoying the sensation of what little breeze there was as it teased its way beneath her rather short dress.

Half a mile or so further on Red found herself at a point in the road where it met with the southernmost tip of the forest. It wasn't far off midday now, and the sun had climbed almost directly above her. She gave the trees a sideways glance as her mother's warning words came back to her, and with a sigh she stomped ever onwards. Red knew well that the road swept east all the way around the edge of the forest, and that with granny living on the most north-westerly point she would be adding a good half-hour, at least, to her journey by following its course. Again she took a look to the left, and could see how wonderfully shaded it looked beneath the pines and the birches as their branches spread out above the forest floor. Yet even then she remained mindful of her mother's instruction, and kicking at a loose stone she forged on.

The sun was excruciatingly hot now and poor Red mopped her sweat-slick forehead with her forearm. She was starting to feel rather hungry too, and dearly wished she'd brought along something to eat. There were granny's provisions, of course, but the poor old dear was ill and it would have been quite wrong of her to help herself to them. And so, finally deciding that desperate times called for desperate measures, she looked quickly up and down the road once more before she quickly ducked away and climbed beneath the wonderful shelter of the trees.

She had to backtrack just a little across the soft, needle-strewn ground, but she found the path quickly enough and it wasn't long before she was so deep within the forest that the dusty road and the baking sun were no longer in her thoughts.

It was certainly dark beneath the boughs of the trees, and Red considered that a person of a nervous disposition might well be feeling a little scared right about now, but she reminded herself that she was a brave girl and pushed on without regret.

A short while later the path opened out onto a clearing carpeted with cornflower, poppy, daisy and flax. Red thought it to be just about the most enchanting place she had ever seen, and heeding her mother's words, if only this once, she quickly set about picking a huge bunch of flowers for her grandmother. She picked and she picked, congratulating herself on being so clever as to find such a place, bending low from the waist and neglecting to consider that she was wearing such a short dress, and with a bare behind too! But why on earth should she care, as she was so clearly alone?

'Well, that's a pretty little posy, I must say,' came a deep, rumbling voice from behind her, and poor Red nearly jumped out of her skin with fright. She immediately stood upright and spun round to see a man sat right behind her, with his enormous back set against an old oak tree. He was casually whittling away at a piece of wood with a pointed blade, and she just stared, absolutely certain that he hadn't been there a moment before. Even though he was sitting the man looked like a giant to Little Red, and she noticed that, despite the heat of the day, he was wrapped in a wolf skin cloak. She looked closer still and saw that his hair was grey-black in colour, and that his cheeks and jaw were heavily stubbled, but for three diagonal lines scored deep into his flesh. She stared into his milky-blue eyes and swallowed awkwardly as she realised exactly who this stranger must be.

'So what brings a pretty little thing like you into the forest, where a big bad wolf could come and gobble you all up?' the man mocked with a wry smile, his knife continuing to slice long, curling shavings from the wood as though it was no harder than a stick of butter.

'Um, I'm going to my granny's house,' Red replied meekly, suddenly aware of just how little she was wearing, and she dipped her head and pulled her dress tight against her naked thighs.

'Well the forest's a dangerous place for a beautiful young lady to be walking. Just you make sure you stick to the path,' he advised.

'Are those flowers for granny?' he asked, to which Red anxiously nibbled her lower lip and nodded her head in response. 'What a kind young lady you are. Your granny is very lucky indeed to have a caring granddaughter such as you.' His voice was as smooth and as seductive as honeycomb drenched in cream. 'But please,' he continued, 'it was rude of me to stop you while you're at work. Do continue.'

Red looked down at the bunch of flowers she clutched to her breasts like a bride on her wedding day. 'I... I think I'm done now,' she offered, in a voice barely more than a whisper.

'Oh, come now, Little Red, I'm sure you love your granny very much and would want her to have a particularly wonderful gift. Look just in front of you, there's a flush of larkspur that would look quite enchanting in amongst that posy.'

Red furrowed her brow. 'H-how do you know my name?' she asked nervously.

'I know many things, Little Red, but you shouldn't be surprised. I've travelled far and I've travelled wide, and have often heard talk of a beautiful young woman with hair as rich as an autumn sunset, with features as smooth and as delicate as a song bird's egg...' he paused to slowly run his eyes over her body, in a way that caused her to release an involuntary shiver despite the heat of the day, '...and with a form more comely than any maid within three counties. And you know what? No matter how far or how wide I wander, there is only ever one name attached to this creature of legend. They call her...' he said, offering a dramatic pause, 'Little Red.

'But perhaps I am wrong,' he continued, in a much more casual tone, 'and you are not the young lady I have heard spoken of?'

Red, utterly consumed by pride, suddenly blurted, 'No, I mean yes, I mean that's me, yes, my name *is* Little Red.'

'Of course you are and of course it is,' the man replied with a smile. 'And do you know what they call me?'

Red dipped her head once more, hardly daring to reply. 'Are... are you the Wolf?' she said, to which the man guffawed loudly, causing a brace of wood pigeon to suddenly take flight and for poor Red to jump once more. But he just offered her a gentle bow of his head and said that she was quite right, and it was a pleasure to make her acquaintance.

'Now,' he said after a slight pause, 'about that larkspur...'

Red looked down at the tiny blue flowers at her feet. The Wolf was quite right, they would look very pretty in granny's posy, but in that dress she was not at all sure she could pick them without compromising her modesty rather severely. 'I think I have enough flowers now, sir,' she said, but the man's expression suddenly darkened and she felt chilled as though a thunder cloud had passed over the sun.

'Go ahead and pick them,' he instructed softly.

'But...'

'Pick them,' he said again, only this time in a tone accompanied by a strange, guttural growl. Slowly Red began to squat down onto her haunches. 'No, not like that,' he said. 'Pick them just as you were doing before.' And in the full knowledge that she would expose herself so badly if she obeyed, yet not daring to discover what he might do to her if she didn't, she turned to face away and proceeded to bend from the waist.

Poor Little Red's heart raced as she felt the hem of her tiny dress begin to ride up her smooth thighs. The larkspur grew on a slight slope that fell away before her, and try as she might there was no way on earth that she could reach down to them without the need to bend even lower still. Red blushed to the sensation of the soft linen pulled tight against the swell of her hips, and she gasped as it suddenly slid up further to reveal the curve of her peachy round bottom. She knew she was fully exposed now, that her pussy was his to observe, nestled as it was between her thighs, and her chest heaved as she began to quickly pull at the flowers while waiting for the Wolf to make his next move.

A moment passed in silence, however, followed by another and then another until finally she drew enough courage to straighten up and to turn around once more – to discover herself to be all alone!

She looked left and she looked right in search of the brute of a man who had forced her to reveal herself so intimately, yet he was nowhere to be seen. She took just a second to catch her breath, before picking up her basket and thrusting her newly picked flowers inside and scurrying out of the clearing without daring to look back.

As she continued on her way she dwelled on her meeting with the Wolf. Part of her felt she must have been a very lucky young lady indeed, to have gotten away so lightly, but part of her felt rather affronted that he hadn't seemed to want her in the same way other men so obviously did. She thought about what he must have been able to see as she bent low to pick the flowers, and wondered why he hadn't tried to take advantage of her. After all, it couldn't be every day that a girl as pretty as she was found wandering alone in the forest.

The more Red thought about it the more confused she became. The Wolf had indicated himself how pretty she was, and she knew just how much the boys liked to look at her naked body, so why hadn't he wanted her too? She stomped along the path, staring at the ground and feeling her disquiet growing with every step she took.

It was the smell that first caused her to look up and take stock of her surroundings. Red had quite forgotten about her hunger, but that wonderful aroma of simmering vegetables, wild herbs and possibly even a little meat drifting through the trees brought it back to her with a vengeance. With rumbling stomach she looked one way and then the other, until she spotted a tiny wisp of blue-grey smoke drifting up through the trees, and immediately she set off towards it. It was not easy going, away from the path, and she stumbled against tangled roots and sharp brambles as she made her way onward. She pushed further and further on, avoiding stinging nettles as best she could, until finally she staggered into a small clearing where she discovered the origin of that enchanting smell.

An old iron pot hung from a chain attached to a wooden tripod above a crackling camp fire, and bubbling away within it was what Red thought to be the most wonderfully fragrant stew she had ever seen.

'Hello?' she called. 'Is anyone here?' She turned through every point of the compass, calling out a greeting each time, yet no reply came. Still her stomach rumbled and she offered a tiny prayer that the owner of the wonderful food was close by, and that he or she might be willing to share a little of it with her. Leaning over the pot she stirred with the wooden ladle standing in it. She shut her eyes and inhaled deeply, identifying wild garlic, sorrel, potatoes and yes, even a little game. Poor Red's belly ached and she called out once more, but again there was no reply.

She knew well that it would be quite wrong for her to simply help herself, but she still had some way to go before reaching granny's house, and as it was such a large pot… and perhaps if she were only to take a little… and maybe whoever had made it wouldn't mind anyway…

It was no good, the smell wafting up from the stew was as powerful as the darkest of dark magic, and so Red lifted the ladle from the pot and raised it to her lips. She blew against the steaming broth and tried her very best to be patient while it cooled, but when she felt as though she might burst if she didn't try just a little, she took a tentative sip and promptly burnt the tip of her tongue.

Despite this, in that instant she felt sure that she'd never tasted anything quite so spectacular, and she soon wolfed down an entire ladle-full before dipping it back into the pot for a second helping, then a third, and then a fourth until finally she felt as stuffed as a goose on Christmas day. It was just then, when she released an accidental and somewhat unladylike belch of satisfaction, that she heard a twig crack underfoot and with a gasp she spun around to see a man walking slowly towards her.

'Please sir,' she gabbled anxiously, 'I hope you don't mind, but I was just passing by and I—!'

Poor Red squealed as her arms were twisted and forced up behind her back. She tried to turn around in order to discover exactly who had grabbed her, but she was held so tightly and it was simply too painful for her to move. She wrestled herself forward, but it was useless and she could only cry, 'Hey!' as she felt her wrists being bound tightly together with a thin cord of some description. She was in terrible trouble, and she knew it.

She looked up once more at the man who continued to step closer and closer towards her, and noticed how he was smiling, yet not in a friendly way. He didn't at all look like a kindly gentleman disposed to sharing his food with a hungry stranger. He was dressed as a hunter, tall, wiry and sharp of feature. She took in his narrow eyes and pointed nose, and decided she did not like the look of him at all.

'Well, well, just look what we've got 'ere, brother,' he sneered, and Red gasped as the man who'd grabbed her from behind stepped into view to take a good look at her. He had the exact same rodent-like features as the other, only his mop of hair was a shade lighter and he stood an inch or two shorter. Where the first reminded her of a weasel, the second was more akin to a rat.

'Indeed, brother,' the second man replied with a thin, reedy voice. 'And I thought we'd had a good morning trapping those three conies, but it looks as though we've caught us a little thief. And a pretty one at that.'

'Oh no, sirs, please,' Red implored, turning from one to the other. 'You quite misunderstand. I'm not a thief at all. I was just on my way to granny's house when I couldn't help but smell your delicious stew. I did try to see if someone was here, honest I did, but...' Poor Red's heart pounded in her chest. She considered making a bolt for it, but she wasn't completely stupid and knew she'd not get far with her hands being tied so tightly behind her back.

'Well if you're not a thief,' began weasel-features, 'I suppose you're planning to pay us for that stew what you stole?'

'Yes, yes of course,' she quickly replied. 'Only, I've got no coin, but,' she was quickly interrupted by the shorter brother before she could explain herself further.

'So you ain't got no money, but you still took what's not yours. I don't know about you, brother, but I call that stealin'.'

The weasel slowly nodded his agreement while looking Red up and down, in a way she did not like one little bit. 'Well, my pretty little thing,' he mused, scratching his whiskered chin, 'if you've got no coin you'd better have another way to pay us, ain't you?'

'Oh, I can think of another way, brother,' the other said, with a wicked glint in his eye.

Red watched as ratty picked up the basket intended for granny and began to rifle through its contents without due care or respect. 'Flowers,' he sneered, tossing the newly picked posy to the ground. 'No good to me. How about you, brother; they'd look lovely in your hair.' The taller one just sniggered in response. 'Apples and pears?' ratty said, pulling out a checked cloth tied with a string. 'Nice enough, but we can scrump as many o' those as we want. Oh wait!' he suddenly announced, and Red looked up eagerly, hoping with all her heart that he had finally found something to repay her debt. 'A fruit loaf,' he said, pulling it from the basket and sniffing it with his pointed nose. 'Mmm, walnut and plum, if I'm not mistaken. One o' my favourites.'

'Yes!' Red declared. 'Everyone says mother's fruit loaf is the best in the village. Take it, take it please.'

But the man just tossed it to the ground and laughed. 'I think not,' he said, fixing her with his beady eyes. 'But hold on,' he gasped, looking once more into the basket. 'What do we 'ave hear then? Now this I *do* like.'

Red watched in horror as he slowly produced her undergarments from within, stretching them out between grubby little hands. The weasel laughed cruelly and Red felt her cheeks flush with the shame of it all.

'Well,' ratty went on, looking her up and down and wetting his lips. 'When I say "I like", I mean I like what is usually all wrapped up in such a pretty little package.'

Red took a stumbling step back as he made a move towards her. 'No, no please,' she implored as he suddenly reached out and yanked her skirt up to reveal her naked pussy.

'Now *that* I like very much,' he drawled, and before Red had a chance to resist he lunged so that his shoulder slammed into her stomach and she felt herself lifted entirely from the ground. Poor Red tried to struggle but with her hands tied behind her back there was only so much she could do.

'The fallen tree, brother!' the weasel cried

excitedly, clapping his hands together and hopping from one foot to the other, and Red felt herself being carried to where a fallen pine lay on the ground. In no time at all she was flipped over and draped facedown across the curve of the trunk.

'No, please,' she wailed, flailing her legs as she felt her dress being pulled up again and her bare buttocks left exposed to their lecherous stares. One of the wicked huntsmen clawed at her ankles and prised her thighs apart, and Red whimpered at the appalling nature of her predicament.

'Well, well, brother,' ratty said. 'That *is* a pretty little one, but no more than a fair trade for our stew, I say. Now, the question is which 'ole do I try first?'

Red sobbed at her wretched state, salty tears spilling down to the forest floor as she lay there awaiting her fate. It was ridiculous; she might have longed to feel a man inside her, but not such an awful one as either of the two disgusting brothers, and not in such a humiliating way.

'Go fetch the goose fat,' he instructed his taller sibling. 'This one's so young and tender I think it may need a little greasing first.'

Red begged they release her one last time but her protests fell on deaf ears, and then she shrieked with shock, lifting herself up as best she could on stomach muscles alone, as a slippery finger made contact with that most secret of little holes.

'This one first, I think,' sneered the rat of a

man viciously. 'It's been an age since I've found a whore willing to give me her most prized possession. Why don't you go make use o' that pretty mouth of hers, brother? And if she so much as dares to use her teeth we'll pull 'em out one by one.'

'No!' Red pleaded to the sight of the sneering weasel stepping before her and loosening the thick belt at his waist. She watched, utterly disgusted, as he drew down his breeches and released his bloated cock. 'Please,' she begged, but he just grinned a gap-toothed grin and leant forward to wind a filthy fist in Red's silky hair, wrenching her head up and back so that she was forced to gasp through the pain and offer her open mouth to him.

The sun was above and behind him now, and because of the tears that stung her eyes she could not easily make out the scene before her, but just as she felt the tip of his cock press against her parted lips, just when she felt something bigger than a fingertip touch the secret entrance to her arsehole – and all for a few ladles of stew – she saw a huge silhouette suddenly rise up before her. With an almighty thud Red felt the weasel's fist suddenly relax its grip on her hair. She looked harder through squinted eyes, but he just stood there with a blank expression on his face, swaying gently from side to side before his knees gave way and he collapsed in a heap on the ground.

Unlike his vile brother, ratty was given advance warning of his fate and offered a pathetic, high-pitched, 'No, please, we were just playin'…!' before he too was silenced with an awful, bone-crunching thud, followed by a thump as he joined his brother on the ground.

Red sniffed away the last of her tears as she listened to what sounded like two sacks of potatoes being dragged through the undergrowth, before she once more heard a familiar voice behind her. 'What did I tell you about sticking to the path, you foolish child?' came the deep, rumbling voice of the Wolf, and it was clear to hear that he was angry.

'I-I know,' she blubbed, 'but…'

'Let's have no more of your excuses, young lady. You might think you're all grown up now, but you're clearly still in need of a good lesson in respecting the advice of your elders.' And with that Red cried out as she felt the enormous flat of his palm come slapping down upon her naked backside. The pain was like none she had known before and she squealed and thrashed with her legs, but the Wolf merely held them in place with a single hand before smacking her again, and this time even harder still.

'Ouch! Ow! Please!' she begged, but the big bad Wolf just ignored her, raining down spank after spank upon her poorly abused bottom. With each loud slap Red would cry out and try to lift herself away, yet there was nowhere for her to go, what with her wrists bound so tightly and with her body draped over that old tree. Each stinging contact of palm against flesh caused her to tense and release the muscles of her backside, in a way that forced her most intimate of areas to grind into the gnarled bark of the pine beneath her. 'Please!' she implored again and again.

'You're a stupid girl, Little Red,' he chastised, striking her with upward strokes now, in a way that lifted both cheeks with every stinging contact. 'Is this really what you wanted?' he questioned. 'To have your body used by vermin like those two?' Red's tears spilt over once more.

The Wolf's punishment was relentless and her sensitive skin burnt like she'd sat on an ant's nest, but then a peculiar thing began to happen; Little Red noticed that with each spank came a second, equally powerful sensation elsewhere within her. It was a feeling she knew well and it thoroughly confused her that it should present itself now. Perhaps it stemmed from a sense of relief that she'd been saved from such an awful fate. Maybe it came from the knowledge that she remained so utterly vulnerable and that her saviour could now simply take her as his reward.

But deep down she knew there was more to it than that, as this unexpected feeling always accompanied the pain elicited by the Wolf's hand and was entirely physical in nature. Poor Red gritted her teeth and gasped with the bittersweet pleasure of her spanking.

'So would it have made you happy, Little Red? Would you have enjoyed having those two men take it in turns to use your body as they pleased? And oh, how they would have enjoyed *you*, Little Red.'

'No, please!' Red gasped as she felt the tip of a

finger press against her grease-smeared rear hole.

'Well is that not what you wanted? Because surely only a simple girl would wander away from the path if it was not trouble she desired.' With each smack Red felt the ring of muscle around her anus twitch against his finger, and in a way that somehow only added to her strange desire.

She squirmed against the tree trunk in an attempt to dislodge his finger, yet in doing so she only succeeded in parting her thighs that little bit wider and accidentally forced him to enter her, just a little way. 'Stop it, please!' she begged, but with nowhere near enough conviction.

'What's that, Little Red, you want me to stop?' he mocked, continuing to spank her. 'Perhaps you should have thought about that before you entered the forest. Perhaps you should have thought about that before you started showing off your pretty body.'

Little Red sniffed and sobbed with self-pity, then suddenly her mouth opened and she gasped, tensing her stomach muscles as she felt his greasy finger slide lower to run against her slit.

'You know what,' he taunted, 'I think you're enjoying this. Maybe I arrived too soon and I should have left you to the hard fucking you would have received from those two. Let's see if that's what you secretly desired, shall we?' and all of a sudden the Wolf pressed his finger against Red's entrance and slid it all too easily within.

'Noooo!' she cried. Of course she hadn't

wanted those awful brothers to make use of her like that, but there was no denying her arousal now as the brute Wolf withdrew his finger and proceeded to rub her pussy lips, smearing them with her own wetness while continuing to spank her over and over again.

'See, Red,' he teased, pressing a knuckle to her clit and rubbing with a circular motion. 'You *are* a bad girl, aren't you? And you're going to get yourself into a lot of trouble one of these days. Who knows, perhaps today will be that day.'

With a final slap that caused Red to squeal indignantly he stepped away.

All was silent and she remained utterly still while she felt his knife slice through the bonds around her wrists. She carefully moved her aching arms forwards until they too lay draped over the tree trunk, using her fingers to soothe where the cruel cord had bitten into her flesh.

She awaited the next inevitable phase of her punishment to begin, certain that he would now take advantage of her young body as it lay over the tree; certain he would finally fuck her ruthlessly for being the foolish girl she so clearly was. Yes, she was nervous, but she would not resist him; it was only fair that he take his prize as he'd saved her from an awful ordeal, but as she craned her neck back, as she slowly lifted herself upright, wiping the remnants of her tears against the back of a hand, as she stood and turned around, she discovered that once again the Wolf was gone.

She could see the two awful brothers, sitting on

the ground back-to-back. They were bound together with a length of hemp rope, their breeches still gathered around their ankles, and they appeared to be fast asleep. Certainly not wishing to wake them she quickly straightened her dress, refilled her basket and headed back towards the forest path, kicking over the pot of stew that had caused all her trouble in the first place.

Poor Little Red. She'd been taught a cruel lesson that deep down even she knew she deserved, but it left her frustrated and wanting with a burning intensity the like of which she had never known.

As she stomped her way along the path she decided that she hated the Wolf. Once again she questioned why on earth he hadn't bothered to just take her. He could have done anything he wished and she would have been quite powerless to resist him. She wouldn't even have told on him and it could have remained their secret, but oh no! Big, bad Wolf was too good for Little Red.

She marched ever onward, kicking at the undergrowth and angrily swatting at any fly that so much as dared to buzz within her reach, determined that she would ask the first woodsman she came across what *he* thought of her naked pussy. But alas, she met no one else.

Finally the trees began to thin and Red could see the meadow grass that lay beyond the forest, and just there, in the distance, a little red and white dot that was granny's house.

'Stupid wolf,' she cursed to herself as she crossed open ground once more, feeling as though her poor body had been wound as tight as a drum. 'I'll show him who needs a lesson!'

As she made her way up the pretty garden path to granny's front door she felt hot, sticky and angry. She gave a quick rap with her knuckles before entering without waiting for a reply. 'Granny dear, where are you? It's me, Little Red, and I've got some goodies for you,' she called, trying to keep the frustration from her voice.

Granny's cottage was made up of two rooms and stood on a single level only. Red was in the living room, which was made up of little more than a small area for preparing food, a table with two chairs, a stove and a rocking chair. She continued through to the rear of the cottage, calling out as she went, 'Granny! Where are you?' She checked the large bed, but it was empty and had been carefully made with fresh linen. A pretty little washstand stood on one side of the room and there was a small door leading out to the garden on the other, but wherever she turned there was absolutely no sign of her grandmother.

Red was beginning to worry, and went back to the living room, wondering where on earth the old dear could be. It was just then that she spotted a note upon the table. It was written in granny's own unmistakeably spidery hand, and she leant over to read.

My dearest Little Red,

Supposing I do not pass you on the road, do

please forgive me for not being home to greet you. I feel much better now and fancy a little trip out to the farm for lunch after all. Anyway, I will no doubt meet you on the way so this note is quite pointless, but should I not, I have asked a friend to stop by later to accompany you home.
All my Love
Granny

'Grrrr!' Little Red growled, stamping her foot on the wooden floorboards. 'Stupid, old bat!' she cursed, before striding back through to the bedroom.

In all her years she had never known a day turn out so badly, but as she looked at the large ceramic bowl upon the washstand she was at least pleased to see there was fresh water in it. Quickly kicking of her shoes and slipping out of her dress, she washed her hot and dusty body all over. The cool water felt good as it ran across her naked breasts, her stomach and on below. With a sigh she began to relax, just a little, and as her hand smoothed its way across the gentle swell of her belly, she thought back to her adventures of that afternoon. For the first time she accepted that she'd had a lucky escape, but she still felt a nagging hunger within, and her fingers slid down between her thighs, with the thought that she might finally satisfy it.

Just then, however, just as she was about to succumb to the gentle caresses of her fingers, and entirely without warning, the back door burst open and in stepped a giant of a man. Red yelped and took three stumbling steps backwards, draping an arm across her breasts and cupping a palm between her thighs in an attempt to cover herself up. In her shock she didn't recognise him at first, as he was no longer wearing a cloak and he was clutching an enormous basket of newly chopped firewood tight to his chest.

'You!' Little Red shouted with anger when she finally realised who it was, to which the Wolf just offered a gentle bow by way of greeting, before he stepped still further into the room. 'Why Grandma,' she said, making absolutely no effort to hide the sarcasm in her voice, 'what a lot of wood you have chopped.'

'All the better to warm the cottage with Little Red,' he replied breezily, striding beyond her and on through to the living area, where he set the firewood down by the stove. Red could see how he was stripped to the waist now, and the way his naked flesh was marked with several pink scars similar to those across his cheek.

She watched him stand upright and turn towards her, yet she made no attempt to get away, holding her ground as he took a stride towards her. 'Why... grandma,' she said again, slower and without really thinking of what she was saying, 'what... what big muscles you have.'

The Wolf continued to pad slowly across the floor, fixing her in the grip of his milky-blue stare. 'All the better to play with pretty girls like you,' he replied, and all of a sudden she gasped to the sensation of his large hands pressing tightly around her waist. He lifted her from the floor as though she was no heavier than a sack of feathers and she cried out, kicking her legs as she was thrown back onto granny's bed. As she lay there panting she gawped up at him, desperately trying to anticipate his next move, forgetting her naked condition. Her nostrils flared and her chest heaved. She swallowed nervously at the sight of the Wolf stepping closer and closer. She had never seen a man who looked quite so strong, so powerful, and it both scared and excited her at the same time. She watched him run the fingers of one hand through his thick mane of hair, and he smirked as he looked down upon her. 'Why, grandma,' she quavered, 'what... what big teeth you have.'

The Wolf suddenly pounced onto the mattress and growled, 'All the better to eat you with,' before wrenching her thighs wide apart with his hands. Little Red squealed with fear, and if he had proceeded to gobble her up like the beast he was she would not have been surprised at all. Yet while the stubble of his beard growth scratched a little against the soft flesh of her inner thighs, it was only the sensation of his tongue exploring every curve of her tight pussy that consumed her senses, and she clawed her fingernails at the eiderdown and threw back her head.

The Wolf lapped Little Red's cunt with a voracious hunger. He was not slow and he certainly wasn't tender, and from time to time he even took to nipping her flesh with his teeth, but only in a way that would cause her to tense without really hurting. Then she'd relax into the bed once more as the tip of his tongue sought her swollen clit, expertly flicking and rolling the tormented little bud.

Red had never known such bliss. It was frantic and it was animalistic and nothing at all like her fantasy of having a handsome farm lad gently lick her pussy while they hid from her father up in the hay loft. As you might well expect from a creature such as the Wolf, there was scarce place for tenderness and Red thrashed upon the bed, crying out over and over again.

'Yessss!' she hissed as she felt the tip of a finger work its way between her pussy lips to enter her, just a little way. She felt it curve against the contour of her body and work back and forth as he sucked her clit. He tongued her deeper now and in a way that caused her breath to catch and bolts of pure pleasure to shoot through her body. She gripped even tighter against the bed linen, dragging it up as she lifted her hips from the mattress to force her cunt harder against his jaw. 'Oh my! Oh Goodness! Oh yes!' she squealed, and finally she could take it no more and, crying out, collapsed under the weight of the most intense orgasm of her life.

With a shuddering sigh she relaxed and collapsed like a rag doll on the bed. She simply laid there, her head turned to one side, her eyes tightly shut and her breasts heaving as she desperately tried to steady her breath.

Eventually, as she felt a huge weight shift at the foot of the mattress, she opened her eyes to watch the Wolf lift himself away. She peered up at him shyly, not at all sure how one should respond after an experience so intimate, and so she remained silent. He stood at the foot of the bed with sturdy legs set apart, wiping his lips against the back of a hand as he stared down at her impassively. Red watched as he kicked off his boots, each one thudding noisily on the floorboards. She bit nervously at a fingernail while his hands worked at the big brass buckle at his waist. She felt her heartbeat quicken as he untied the leather thong that laced his deerskin breeches together, and finally, she gasped as he pulled them down his enormous thighs.

'Oh, my!' she gasped. 'What a big... what a big cock you have...'

One corner of his mouth twitched into a smug smile before he replied, 'All the better to fuck you with.'

Once again he knelt on the foot of the bed, his impressive shaft gripped tight within a fist. 'But before I do, let's see if that pretty mouth of yours is good for anything other than making excuses, shall we?'

Red didn't know whether to be offended or not, but he towered over her and she was in no position to argue, even if she had wanted to. Slowly, and a little awkwardly, she climbed up onto her knees. She began by allowing her fingertips to run across his chest, and gasped at how hard it felt. She scratched her fingernails lower against the contours of his abdominal muscles, and then down to the thick thatch of hair below. Her hands continued further, until tentatively she took his balls in one palm and closed a fist around his stiff, throbbing cock. Little Red's heart raced as she felt the considerable weight of his balls and how they tightened within her grip. She marvelled at just how smooth his stalk felt as she trailed soft fingertips lightly up and down. She was nervous, she had never performed such an act before, but she'd secretly watched many times, so with a last anxious shiver she leant down between his thighs.

She pressed her lips against the swollen, scarlet head of his prick. She only kissed it at first, tasting his sticky pre-cum on the tip of her tongue, before she took him a little deeper, opening her mouth wide to accommodate his significant girth. She began to suck with hollowed cheeks. She used her tongue to explore the thick ridge at the crown of his cock, her hand gripped tightly around it, her thumb and fingers unable to meet, such were his dimensions. The Wolf released a deep, rumbling growl from the back of his throat and Red looked up through wide eyes, scared that she might have done something wrong, but she saw by the way he held back his head, by the way he shut his eyes tightly, that she was almost certainly doing everything right.

In time she dared to take him a little deeper and work her hands on him too, drawing his foreskin back and forth with one while the other stroked the soft flesh beneath his balls. She listened to his every gasp and moan and tempered her ministrations accordingly, so that in no time at all he was grunting with a greater intensity. Little Red's head bobbed up and down and despite the fact that her jaw was beginning to ache, she discovered her own arousal pulsating between her thighs once more. As she sucked and slurped on the Wolf's enormous shaft she considered that soon she would feel it inside her, and although there was nothing she wanted more, the idea alone caused her heartbeat to race.

'Mmm, you're doing very well, Little Red,' he purred as he wound his fists into her silky soft hair, pulling her still lower onto him and grinding his hips back and forth. Poor Red began to worry that she might choke if he dared to enter her any deeper, but it also felt strangely satisfying to be used solely for the pleasure of another. She felt his prick twitch and spasm within her mouth, and wondered if now would be her chance to experience a man spurting down her throat, but just as he released a rumbling growl of pleasure he lifted her startled face away and his thick cock, glistening with her saliva, plopped from her mouth completely.

The time had finally come, and like a giant beast stalking its prey the Wolf crawled over her on hands and knees, pressing his naked chest against her breasts so that she had no option but to lie back on the mattress, pinned between it and his considerable bulk. With one hand he parted her thighs wide, and she made no effort to resist him.

She gasped nervously as the tip of his cock

touched the flushed swell of her mound. She felt him draw up and down, smearing it with her own moisture and lubricating the head before he settled it against her entrance. Slowly he began to push, and Little Red shut her eyes tight with fear, drawing short breaths as she felt her body begin to yield. Her pussy lips stretched wide around the swelling head of his prick, but for such a beast of a man he was remarkably gentle. He pulled back two or three times to allow her to relax a little. She had never felt anything quite like it as he pushed deeper and deeper with every forward movement, and at the point where she felt as though she'd be torn in two if she was stretched any further, when her head swam with a heady mix of discomfort and bliss, the Wolf suddenly released a mighty howl and sank deep within her.

Poor Little Red cried out, her inner muscles convulsing against his stout shaft as he held still, buried in her to the hilt. Beyond the shock of the moment she gasped at how wonderful it felt to be penetrated so completely.

In time the Wolf drew slowly back until the thick ridge of his cock began to pull at her entrance once more, before he powered forward again, causing her to cry out with bliss-filled pleasure. The Wolf fucked Little Red with long smooth strokes of his giant shaft, and she angled her hips to accept him fully.

'Oh, God!' she cried, even though she knew it was particularly wrong to blaspheme on a Sunday. But she simply couldn't help herself, and we must forgive her as the sensation of his outrageous cock pumping in and out was so much more than she had ever imagined it could be, and without thinking she raked her fingernails deep into the flesh of his back until even he was forced to curse and rise up on his arms.

'Oh, fuck!' she shrieked, shutting her eyes and biting her lower lip. 'Fuck me! Fuck me harder, Mr Wolf!' and the Wolf dutifully obliged.

He took her ankles in his giant fists and lifted her legs high and wide apart so that her bottom was lifted from the bed and she was forced to cry out with desperate sobs of pleasure. He withdrew completely and flipped her onto her front, before entering her from behind in a way that allowed her to imagine she was one of the whores from the village, or better still, that she was being taken against her will. And just when she felt her second climax begin to swell, he threw her onto her back again, sinking his wet erection deep inside her again.

The Wolf thrust and Little Red gasped to the wonderful joy of being fucked so thoroughly at last. Her orgasm overwhelmed her, and her scream of delight caused startled birds on the fringes of the forest to take flight. She had never known pleasure quite like it, but then gradually, inevitably, she began to slow and her awareness returned to a level where she could watch and feel the Wolf finding his own ultimate release deep within her weary body.

For a time they were still, hearts racing,

exhausted. Little Red drew in the salty scent of his fresh sweat, proud that she'd given him such pleasure. Eventually the Wolf rolled to one side with a grunt and she rather cheekily threw out an arm so that her hand could rest upon his sticky, semi-erect prick.

A short while later, and with no little disappointment, she watched as he climbed from the bed. He stood before her, naked and unabashed, and she couldn't help but eye his mighty cock hanging between those trunk-like thighs, and she dearly wanted to play with it some more.

'Time to get you back home, Little Red,' he said. 'Your family will be wondering where you've got to, and as it'll be a full moon this night, there's no telling what beasts will be out there with a taste for fresh blood.'

Red gave him a sideways glance to check that he was joking, but he ignored her and set about dressing. Releasing a sudden involuntary shiver she agreed that perhaps it was indeed time for them to leave, and climbed off the bed to wash and dress too.

Like a good girl she changed the bed linen and found a clay jug to arrange the wild flowers in, while the Wolf set fresh firewood in the hearth for granny.

They took the long way back by the road, but it was much cooler now, and in a way she wanted to take her time. She had so much she wanted to ask him, about his travels, and if any of the stories people told about him were true, but for once she was just happy being silent, and so they walked on without sharing a word, enjoying the first signs of sunset painting the sky with purple and gold.

Once they reached the boundary of her father's farm they stood still. 'Would you like to come and share some food?' Red asked, a little shyly. 'I'm sure there'll be plenty left over from lunch.' The Wolf just smiled and shook his shaggy head.

Red turned and looked towards her little house in the distance, the first oil lamps already burning from within, and she knew he was right. He would not be welcomed.

Spinning round to say a final goodbye and to ask if she might see him again, Little Red gasped to discover that she was all alone once more. This time she didn't bother to look for where he might be, as she knew well that he was gone, yet perhaps still watching.

And so, dear reader, as Little Red wound her way up the tree-lined path to her home, we reach the end of our tale. Does it finish with a happily-ever-after? Well in a way I suppose it does, only perhaps not in the way you might expect. Red did not marry the Wolf and they did not settle down in the forest to raise a little pack of their own. In the same way as a wolf will always be a wild killer at heart, no matter how carefully you train it, Little Red would always be Little Red. It was in her nature, and it wasn't long before she was back to her old tricks and enjoying herself as before.

I could go on to tell you about how she soon

sought those boys who had once paid her brother to watch as she bathed, to offer them so much more if they gave their money directly to her instead.

I could let you know that the very next time she led a little audience to watch her swim naked in the creek, she marched straight up to where they lay hidden and demanded they touch her inappropriately or else she would tell her father they'd been spying on her.

I could tell you that on that very next Friday evening, when the farmhands returned drunk from the tavern, Little Red came knocking at their door to show them she was not so 'little' any more.

Maybe I could even tell you how that following summer, when once more the travellers came to work the fields, she allowed them to persuade her that, where they came from, it was quite normal for a pretty young lady, such as she, to suck their cocks one after the other, until her body was rendered little more than a sticky mess.

I could even go on to let you know that, when the mood took her, Little Red could be found wandering alone in the forest with a bare bum and short dress in the hope that she might stumble across wicked men who might tie her up and use her young body until she would be forced to beg for mercy.

These are all tales for another day, however, and ones I will gladly tell; all you need do is find me…